Arrabella had a dogged determination in her formative years to succeed in life. Her favourite academic subject was English literature. She was also very successful on track and field, representing her school and athletics club. Her ambitions were put on hold abruptly through personal family trauma. She never gave up on her goals, gaining an LLB degree and master's in law at university as a mature student. She has held down several professional roles in the legal profession and the police constabulary. She works as a mentor, supporting international students. Arrabella has a 'can do' approach and uses every obstacle that she's faced in life as a challenge to turn into a positive outcome. Her hobbies include, writing, gardening, walking, antiques, and meeting new people.

I would like to dedicate this manuscript to my dear mother, (now deceased) 'Miss Ville' as she is affectionately known by her family, for giving me the determination to believe in myself, and in her words to 'aim high'. I hope that she would have been proud of me if she was alive today to see my manuscript in print.

Arrabella Williams

A FOOT IN BOTH CAMPS

AUSTIN MACAULEY PUBLISHERS™

LONDON • CAMBRIDGE • NEW YORK • SHARJAH

A CIP catalogue record for this title is available from the British Library.

ISBN 9781398431461 (Paperback)
ISBN 9781398431478 (ePub e-book)

www.austinmacauley.com

First Published 2022
Austin Macauley Publishers Ltd®
1 Canada Square
Canary Wharf
London
E14 5AA

I would like to acknowledge following people for their support in writing my short story. My sister, Andrea, for her patience and encouragement. My good friend, Graham Paskett, for his unwavering encouragement and proof reading my manuscript over the years. AM Publishers, for their absolute professionalism in making this publication happen with their expert team. Lastly, but not least, I would like to thank my son, Lee, for his unwavering belief in me.

Introduction

A Snapshot of Daily Life in the Fletchers' Household

Susie's father Mr Solomon Fletcher was a very hard-working manual worker who would usually leave the house very early in the morning and return home in the early hours of the evening. He worked at the local steel works as a labourer. Susie was often awoken in the early hours most mornings to the sound of Radio 4, with the world's events blasting out loudly in their quiet sleepy household, invading her dreams intermittently as she drifted in and out of sleep.

Mr Solomon Fletcher was very proud of his cultural roots and heritage – which he had instilled into his children. He stressed the importance of keeping one's identity. He had always said that he was not going to change who he was, or the way that he spoke for anyone... and insisted that the indigenous population in the UK would have to be made to understand his language, which was a combination of 'Pigeon English' and 'Patois'. Mr Solomon Fletcher spoke with a very thick Jamaican accent, which became very difficult to understand whenever he became angry because his speech would accelerate, which would annoy Mrs Ruby Fletcher and went against the grain of her efforts to instil proper grammar and dialect in their children. The difference in child rearing between Susie's parents, who would often be heard arguing about the 'rights and wrongs' of what culture took precedence in their children's lives.

"But Sister Ruby," – Susie's father would plead in one of his many arguments with Susie's mother – "the children are Jamaican and shouldn't be ashamed about who they are."

Mrs Ruby Fletcher would also argue back in reply, "I know that Brother Fletcher, but we live in the UK and our children are English."

"They are born here in England."

"They shouldn't speak Patois, which is 'Pigeon English', it's not a proper language. They will not be able to progress at school with their education and wouldn't be taken seriously by their teachers and school friends. Our children would be placed in the 'C' classes which would be the lowest class in their school system."

Susie's parents always referred to each other as 'Brother' and 'Sister', which was the norm and acceptable way for married couples and members of their Evangelical Church to address each other. Susie hadn't known it any other way. In fact, at one point, when she was much younger, Susie became quite confused and thought that her parents were biological brothers and sisters, when she first noticed that her parents were referring to each other as, 'Brother' and 'Sister'.

The conflict between Susie's parents in terms of what culture that should take precedence in their children's lives was like a simmering volcano that was always bubbling under the surface, and it didn't take much prodding for the volcano to erupt at unexpected times between Susie's parents. The conflict in the home would be compounded when Mr Solomon Fletcher bought the weekly 'Jamaican Gleaner', which was a Jamaican newspaper, which kept the 'homesick', Mr Solomon Fletcher abreast and up to date with what was happening in his homeland… which seemed so far away. Mr Solomon Fletcher would comment aloud as he read the Gleaner newspaper,

"Oh dear!" Mr Solomon Fletcher would exclaim in a surprised tone. "De Dollar has gone down against de pound again."

"De Government is not doing enough to help the poor families in J.A" – which was Mr Solomon Fletcher's abbreviation for Jamaica.

Susie would browse through the newspaper and read aloud the comical and humorous words in the black and white cartoon captions which had drawings of people commenting on the Current Affairs that had hit the Jamaican headlines in the Caribbean Island.

"De Government says dat de price of gasoline has gone up."

"This means that we are going to have to leave Jamaica and immigrate to England to find work in order to feed our pickneys."

Susie's mother would interrupt and scold her while she was reading in midsentence,

"Speak properly Susie!" She said. "I don't want you reading the Jamaican Gleaner Newspaper and speaking patois."

"It's not good for your English Grammar."

"Why can't you read your Peter and Jane Ladybird books, which would help you with your English Grammar at School?"

The conflict between Mr and Mrs Ruby Fletcher's differences in their children's values and culture was always the bone of contention in the Fletchers' house which made Susie feel that she literally had her 'foot in both camps', taking bits of the values from both of her parents.

Chapter 1

Breakfast Time: A Family Affair in the Fletchers' House

As would usually happen in the Fletchers' Anglo Caribbean household, breakfast would consist of Corn Meal porridge which was prepared by Mrs Ruby Fletcher for Susie and her five other siblings. The corn meal porridge had the appearance of yellow sand mixed with milk, which would simmer away gently on the gas stove, (in the dimly lit kitchen), gently for about thirty minutes then sweetened with condensed milk and nutmeg, exuding a very warm homely ambiance around all the rooms in the small-town house. Susie's mother would cook the corn meal in a large stainless-steel pot. When cooked the corn meal would have the deceptive appearance of being cool, but in reality, it would burn into their tongues as though it was being burnt with a hot poker taken from the earthen grate in the kitchen by the stove.

Susie's mother would use an enamel cup in which to shovel the piping hot corn meal porridge into their respective bowls, helped along by a wooden spoon. Susie and Freddie would often fight over whose turn it was to scrape off the stuck-on corn meal from off the large stainless-steel pot, which tasted of sweet toffee apple mixed with condensed milk.

Although Susie was not a huge fan of corn meal porridge at breakfast times, she told herself that it was much better than having to go on 'fasting', which would invariably happen once a month, when her parents would go without breakfast and also instruct Susie and her four other siblings that they would also not be allowed food for the three hours that they would be at their Evangelical Church services, which in the early days… took place in the Fletchers' front room.

The hunger pangs that would rip through Susie's stomach was indescribable. Prior to eating breakfast and at all mealtimes, Susie and her four siblings would religiously sing a 'thank you' prayer to God for their food, prior to eating their meal, which they would recite, with their hands clasped together and their eyes firmly closed, which went along the lines;

'Thank you for the world so sweet.

Thank you for the food we eat.

Thank you for the birds that sing.

Thank you, God, for everything.

Amen,

For what we are about to receive.

May the Lord make us truly grateful.'

Mrs Ruby Fletcher prevented Susie and her siblings from talking whilst they were eating their meals at the table. She would expect from her children impeccable table manners, and would often firmly tell her brood that they, 'shouldn't talk with your mouth full', and that they should 'ask to be excused from the table if you wanted to go'. Mrs Ruby Fletcher would also scold her children for talking too fast. Susie's mother would often say to her and her siblings, 'you must speak properly', or 'you're speaking too fast', and sometimes say, 'slow down!' She would often say to her children, "When you go to school the teacher won't be able to understand you if you speak 'Patois'. You must speak proper English."

Mr Solomon Fletcher, however, was the complete opposite to their mother and would often be heard correcting Mrs Ruby Fletcher, whilst in the living room as he heard Mrs Ruby Fletcher attempt to change her accent whenever she spoke to a white person. "Speak your own language!" He would shout at the top of his voice when Susie's mother was standing at the front door, having small talk with the milkman, and attempting without success to speak the Queen's English in her Jamaican accent, whilst paying the family's weekly milk bill.

Although Susie was only four years old, she was quite tall for her age with a slender frame. Susie had big brown eyes which made a lovely contrast with her cocoa skin which glistened on a sunny day. Mrs Ruby Fletcher was a seamstress, and she would invariably dress Susie in brightly coloured flowery dresses which Susie would wear, unaware of the endless hours that Mrs Ruby Fletcher spent sewing away on her large black sewing machine.

Being the first girl to be born in the Fletcher household, Susie was treated like a little doll by her mother who had longed for a little girl after having given birth to two older brothers, Freddie aged six years and Kingsley aged twelve years who had recently joined the family from Jamaica. Susie also had two younger siblings… Carlton aged three years and Ruby aged two years. Therefore, having Susie as her first daughter 'was an answer to prayer', she said. Susie was very attached to her mother. Mrs Ruby Fletcher would comb and plait Susie's hair placing several ribbons in her long thick locks. She would be dressed up in frilly 'ballerina' looking dresses which Susie would wear to the yearly garden parties and whenever Mrs Ruby Fletcher took her out and otherwise, she would also wear a different coat for every occasion. For example, Susie would wear a blue coat for trips to the butchers and wore a cream coat for outings to the local market.

Susie was a determined, strong-willed girl who would try Mrs Ruby Fletcher's patience on many occasions, which inevitably led to a clash of wills between the two females in the Fletcher household. Mrs Ruby Fletcher would tell Susie in no uncertain terms who was the boss, shouting in a loud stern voice,

"There's only one woman in this house! You're still a 'pickney' and you will do as you're told!"

Susie would fold her arms and defiantly stamp her feet as she walked quickly up the steep uncarpeted stairs towards her bedroom.

Mrs Ruby Fletcher was short in stature but a large bosom woman with plump arms and legs that created a rustling noise whenever she walked. Her complexion was a lighter shade of brown to that of her children. When she smiled, her beaming plump face would reveal shinny white ivory teeth which revealed a split in the centre of her top row. Her bosom was always a source of comfort for Susie and her siblings, whenever they felt tired or in need of comfort. In the house, Mrs Ruby Fletcher always dressed in a bright yellow apron with long sleeves, with a multi-coloured head scarf tied neatly around her head with two plaits sticking out at the base of the tightly secured scarf. She was a very kind-hearted and gentle woman who could be heard around the house singing 'spiritual songs!' Mrs Ruby Fletcher regularly sang,

"This peace that I have, the world didn't give it to me,"

"The world didn't give it; the world can't take it away."

Susie was very similar to her mother and loved singing, and her high-pitched voice could be heard up and down the large four bedroomed Victorian house. One of Susie's favourites songs that she often sang much to her parents' displeasure was the song that she had learned whilst at school, which she would belt out, that went along these lines,

"My Bonnie flew over the ocean,

My Bonnie flew over the sea,

My Bonnie flew over the ocean,

Go bring back my Bonnie to me!"

Susie's father, Mr Solomon Fletcher was a very strict Christian man, who would invariably scold Susie when she sang this song. He would often shout at her with his deep baritone Caribbean voice,

"Susie… stop singing that 'wrong song' in de house!"

"Where did you learn that song from?"

Susie would stop singing instantly but would defiantly hum the song under her breath in protest against Mr Solomon Fletcher's objection.

Mr Solomon Fletcher would view all songs that didn't refer to God in the verses as being, 'wrong songs of the world', in his eyes.

Susie and her siblings feared their father because although there were moments when he would laugh and was often amusing, he was also very strict and would use a leather belt as a form of discipline on his children if he felt that their behaviour warranted it. In the Caribbean culture, they were told that this form of punishment was discipline. Mr Solomon Fletcher would recite verses from the bible to back up his theory on strict discipline. He would often say, "The wise man Solomon stated in one of his proverbs, 'Do not spare the rod and spoil the child'." He would say in his thick Jamaican accent.

Mr Solomon Fletcher was an exceptionally tall well-built man with a very deep voice… who towered over Susie and her siblings. His skin was of a cool dark brown complexion with a large busy moustache that almost covered his brown top lip. He had a gold tooth in the middle at the top of his front teeth which glistened when he opened his mouth. Mr Solomon Fletcher's daily attire consisted of a large dark blue overall, a brown chequered flat cap, with black slippers.

Although he was a manual worker, Mr Solomon Fletcher would dress very smartly for Church which took place at Susie's house on a Sunday morning. Mr Solomon Fletcher wore pristine linen shirts with matching ties. His suits were also well made with the best material from the local suit fitters. Susie had only seen her father wearing a black suit on the very rare occasions when he attended a funeral. His suits were a combination of greys, and brown checked material. His ties were an assortment of numerous colours. The shoes that he wore were made of very strong brown leather and had an array of patterns and zig zags dotted around the front and tips of his toes.

Susie's brother Freddie was six years old, two years older than Susie herself. Freddie was quite tall in stature and his body was quite broad with a large face similar to Mr Solomon Fletcher's. His skin tone was a combination of his parents, with different and contrasting shades of cool dark brown on his face and a lighter shade of brown on his arms and legs. Mrs Ruby Fletcher would dress Freddie in a blue checked shirt with grey shorts with blue braces which were rather tight on his shoulders, giving the impression of a puppet on a very tight string. Freddie was a quiet child in contrast to his sister Susie. Freddie was a solitary child and spent most of his time when not at school in the house and the garden, pretending to be a bus driver with his imaginary passengers on board. He would use the pot covers from Mrs Ruby Fletcher's kitchen for the wheel of his bus and would make indistinct noises, 'Brum, Brum, Brum'. "Let's go," Freddie would shout. Freddie was happiest when playing this game. Mrs Ruby Fletcher would often say to Mr Solomon Fletcher that Freddie would become a bus driver when he grew up.

Susie's male siblings would be treated by Mr Solomon Fletcher as having a superior position in the family home. Mr Solomon Fletcher would forbid Freddie and his three brothers from going into the kitchen to help with the domestic chores. "Get out of the kitchen Freddie!" Mr Solomon Fletcher would exclaim loudly. "Boys shouldn't be in the kitchen." Mr Solomon Fletcher's bias towards 'men and women' roles, was non-negotiable and fixed. Mrs Ruby Fletcher's opinion was of no significance to her husband, nor did he take any notice of Mrs Ruby Fletcher's objection or challenge to Mr Solomon Fletcher's point of view, which would leave Susie feeling of no significance invisible and of low self-worth. There was definitely a demarcation of the role of men and women in the Fletchers' household. The Fletcher household was very male dominated with Mr Solomon Fletcher taking the position as the head of the house and that was it; with Mrs Ruby Fletcher, Freddie and the Fletcher children taking the back seat. Mr

Solomon Fletcher was the man of the house, and his decision was final.

Chapter 2

The Early Years

Susie was three years old when she had her earliest memories whilst living in Northampton. Her parents were among the thousands of immigrants who had dared to venture the treacherous seas and boarded the Empire Windrush which carried hundreds of Caribbean people at a time to the UK in order to get a better life, after the British government in power at the time were asking for people to come from the 'Motherland', Jamaica to work as a source of cheap labour. The Fletchers settled in an East Midlands Town called Northampton, where many immigrants from the Caribbean migrated because they were told there was plenty of work available in the steel works, being one of the main industries that was short on cheap labour. Susie, Carlton, Ruby, Freddie and baby Benjamin were all born in Northampton, with the exception of Kingsley who was born in Jamaica.

The Fletchers lived in a dilapidated four bedroomed Victorian house with an attic at the top of the house. There was a tall cast iron gate which separated the house from the pavement. Inside the gate was a large metal grate which covered the area where the coal was emptied into a large hole into the dark dusky cellar underneath the house. There were a further four steep steps that the Fletcher children had difficulty stepping onto due to having such small feet. The front of the house had paint peeling off its black wooden door on various places. Inside the hallway which smelt musty was a hard stone patterned tiled floor in colours of reds, greens, blue and black. The high ceiling in the hallway and the rest of the house created a sharp icy draft when the front door was opened. All the rooms in the house had very high ceilings which gave the rooms a cold icy greeting when the doors were opened. There were three rooms downstairs, which consisted of a large kitchen which was situated to the rear of the house. The kitchen exuded a warm spicy nutmeg ambience as one entered the kitchen. The window in the kitchen was rather small in comparison to the large kitchen. A worn looking black well-used gas stove which occupied a small corner had the appearance of having seen better days. The kitchen was the place where Mrs Ruby Fletcher prepared the family's meals. It was the only place that she had peace and quiet to escape from the hustle and bustle of the family home. A large dark wooden table graced the uncarpeted wooden floor. It was supported in the middle by two of its four wooden legs that folded in the middle when not in use. The heat from the small coal fire in the far centre corner of the kitchen gave a cosy inviting feeling, which was a good distraction from the cold bricked walls. There would always be a large metal fireguard around the belching coal fire. Mrs Ruby Fletcher would place the family's damp clothes onto a wooden clothes horse next to the fire guard in order to dry them.

The bathroom was situated at the back of the kitchen, which meant that one had to walk through the kitchen in order to get into the bathroom. The dimly lit cold damp bathroom was very small in comparison to the rest of the rooms downstairs and was not big enough to swing a cat. The walls were painted an off grey colour which was peeling off in various places. The bath resembled a stained off-white oversized basin with grease mark stains on the inside. There were several small metal buckets with handles and lids which the Fletcher family and the lodger families used as a lavatory in their bedrooms during the night because the only lavatory was situated outside at the back of the house.

The second room was a small living room where the Fletcher children would sit avidly watching 'Captain Scarlet' and 'Thunderbirds' their favourite children's television programmes. In the centre of the room was a large round dark wooden table with five mismatched chairs. The stone floors were bare with a small rug at the doorway. Mr Solomon Fletcher had his own special seating, where no one was allowed to sit, which was a worn spring-less brown material lined settee that sunk in the middle whenever Mr Solomon Fletcher sat down onto it. On the wall was a gold frame with a red background. The words in the frame were written in black, which read,

"God is the Head of this house, the unseen Guest at **every** meal, the silent **Listener** to **every conversation.**" These words always gave the Fletcher children a feeling of intense unease, as they imagined God being sat next to them whilst they would talk about antics that they had got up to as children at school, that their parents would disagree with.

The front room was the 'best' room in the Fletchers' house, which was situated at the front of the house and was out of bounds for the Fletcher children to go into, or any children for that matter. In this 'out of bounds', 'sacred' room, (which was the smallest room downstairs), lived the Bible which was always left open. The bible had large letterings with very scary coloured paintings of angelic creatures with wings floating upon white clouds. There was a three pieced suite in the front room, which was dark brown in colour, or so it looked because it was always covered in plastic in order to keep it clean for whenever Susie's parents had visitors around and for when the Fletchers held their Sunday Services. The carpet was pristine in appearance, with a variety of colours red, green and yellow floral patterns. The wallpaper was gold and white.

The front room would be the place where the Fletchers' would entertain their friends who would visit the family, and also their Church Brethren would be led into the front room on a night during the week when they held their prayer meetings. The Fletcher children would only be allowed to go into the front room when their parents held their Sunday morning and evening services.

The bare wooden steep stair way that leads to the bedrooms upstairs was very cold and uninviting as the Fletcher children didn't wear shoes in the house and didn't possess any slippers which would have protected their small delicate feet from the cold rough surface of the bare floor.

Susie and Ruby shared the smallest room with a single double-bed because there were two other Caribbean families who also occupied two other rooms with their children. Their bedroom was situated at the back of the house. In the room a small dark wooden dressing table with a large mirror that bent at the hinges. The double bed had metal springe bases which the Fletcher children would playfully jump up and down onto. The bedding was sparse with a thick ribbed heavy blue sheet and two brown pillowcases filled with old clothes. The Fletcher children didn't wear pyjamas at bedtime. Instead, they would wear their old clothes that they had grown out of that were ripped and were no longer worn in the house.

The two Fletcher brothers (except for baby Benjamin who slept in a large wooden cot in his parents' room) all shared a room slightly bigger than Susie and Ruby, which was situated at the back of the house. There was no other furniture in the bedroom apart from the sparsely furnished double bed that the Fletcher brothers shared.

On the next landing was Mr and Mrs Ruby Fletchers bedroom, that was situated at the front of the house which was 'out of bounds' to the Fletcher children, who were not allowed to venture into under any circumstances. However, being the determined young girl that Susie was, she had on occasions encouraged her older brother Freddie to accompany her, and both had crept into their parent's room when Mrs Ruby Fletcher was downstairs taking care of Ruby the youngest girl in the Fletcher household or doing the household chores, and Mr Solomon Fletcher was out at work during the day. Their parents' room was much bigger than the room that she shared with Ruby and also that of her brothers. However, their bedroom appeared 'grander' with a metal bed headboard at the top and bottom of the bed. The double bed was dressed in heavier dark green bed linen. There was a large dark brown wooden dressing table next to the large window that looked down onto the cobbled streets.

Freddie didn't like entering into his parents' bedroom because he had an extreme phobia about Mrs Ruby Fletcher's brown stockings that were draped over the headboard at the bottom of the bed. His mother's room also gave him the creeps and ran shivers down his spine to the extent that he would cry and scream profusely and loudly jumping on the spot in terror, as Mrs Ruby Fletcher's stockings appeared to sway backwards and forwards on the headboard.

"Mammie, mammie. Aargh, aargh!"

Freddie's screams would alert Mrs Ruby Fletcher who was downstairs in the kitchen to the commotion upstairs. Mrs Ruby Fletcher would shout,

"Susie, what's the matter with Freddie?"

Susie would reply to Mrs Ruby Fletcher in a loud pitched shrill, her voice cracking with fits of laughter, and almost drowned out by Freddie's very high-pitched shrieks of terror his foot stomping.

"Freddie is frightened of your stockings in your bedroom."

"What did I tell you children? Didn't your daddy tell you not to go into our bedroom?"

"You just wait 'til your daddy gets home from work tonight! You're going to get such a beating tonight!"

The Fletchers had two sets of Caribbean lodgers who occupied the fourth bedroom, and the attic bedroom at the top of the house on the next landing. Both bedrooms had keys which were always locked which meant that their privacy was protected from the prying eyes of the Fletcher children who were unable wander into.

The garden where Susie, her siblings and the lodgers' children played was a small strip of concreted surface which was situated at the back of the house. There was a small, grassed area at the back of the garden which was used as a rubbish tip consisting of the Fletcher family's old clothes with branches from a large old tree in the garden, to get the fire started.

Susie would spend endless hours bouncing her red and blue ball against the wall of the house, reciting songs that she had learned whilst at school, chanting words along the lines of,

"In Leicester Square,
There is a school,
And in that school,
There are some classes,
And in those classes,
There are some desks,
And in those desks,
There are some books.
And in those books,
There are some,
A, B, C, D, E, F."

Susie's mother Mrs Ruby Fletcher would have to shout Susie to come into the house for her tea on many occasions, because Susie would be lost in her own world of singing whilst bouncing her red and blue balls against the wall of the house.

Chapter 3

Church Services in the Fletchers' House

The first lodger family was named the Stirling family who had two small girls aged around nine and ten years old. The second family were named the Wright who had three boys aged four, seven and nine years old. Both families along with the Fletchers were Christians. All the families in the house including the Fletchers would all get together to have a church service which would take place in the Fletchers' house on a Sunday morning and evening. These services would be very loud spirit filled affairs, where there would be a lot of loud praying, singing and jumping around the living room. Susie would get very scared and would cower next to her mother holding onto her dress tightly, pleading to be picked up and comforted, but to no avail because she too had her eyes closed and her hands raised up into the air.

"Praise the Lord!" The families would shout at the top of their voices.

Susie and the children would find some of the behaviour of the adults in attendance and taking part in the home church services hilarious and would burst out laughing uncontrollably. The women would jump around in these services in a spiritual trance with their eyes tightly closed with their hats falling off in disarray.

The very noisy Sunday Home church services attracted numerous police visits after a period of time as a result of complaints from the Fletcher's English neighbours. The police would ask Susie's parents to keep the noise down. Susie's mother would say to the policeman in defence,

"But we're only praying to our Lord! The bible says we should make a joyful noise to the Lord!"

Susie's mother was told by the policeman that because they lived in a quiet residential area the neighbours objected to being woken up in the early hours of the morning on a Sunday when they were having a lie in after working six days a week. The neighbours also objected to services being kept on a Sunday evening when they were trying to settle their young children for an early night, ready for school the next day.

Susie's parents were told in no uncertain terms that if the noise persisted, then they would lose their tenancy, with notice to find alternative accommodation. This warning worried Susie's parents. Susie's mother said that she would, "Pray and fast about the situation." She said that they were not going to give up worshipping their God, and went about in search of alternative accommodation, and a landlord who would be sympathetic and understanding to their Christian way of life.

Chapter 4

The Fletcher Family on the Move

Susie had overheard her parents in conversation saying that moving house had not come easy because many of the houses that were available to rent had notices which was written in capital letters on the front of the doors and windows with the words stating, 'No BLACKS, NO IRISH and NO DOGS'. Susie's father wondered how he would ever be able to move house with such obstacles in the family's path. Mr Solomon Fletcher would say in despair,

"We have to put our trust in God. Only our Father God in heaven can help us."

Mr Solomon Fletcher recalled and spoke about several upsetting incidents where he had responded to various adverts in the local Northampton newspaper, which had advertised various properties with vacant rooms to rent. However, when he had visited the property, on answering the front door, the white Landlord on seeing that Mr Solomon Fletcher was in fact a black immigrant had told him that the rooms had already been taken and that there were no rooms available to rent. Mr Solomon Fletcher would say that he didn't believe that the rooms had been taken because the advert had just been placed in the Northampton Mail newspaper in many cases on the same morning and could not have been filled by tenants that early. Also, Susie's father said that he could tell when someone was not genuine or was lying by looking into their eyes. He said that he was never fooled by their, 'smiling thirty-two teeth'. Susie was unaware at the time that one's full set of teeth consisted of thirty-two teeth. Mr Solomon Fletcher would say that some of the landlords would yell at him, shouting,

"Go back to your own country!" And would slam the door on him, without even telling him whether they had vacant rooms to rent. Other landlords would just stare at him in shock, smiling nervously as they opened the door, and would tell Mr Solomon Fletcher that the last three rooms had just been filled, but their eyes would say otherwise.

These experiences Mr Solomon Fletcher called, 'Colour Bar', left him feeling dejected, isolated, and homesick. At the time Susie had no idea what the words 'Colour bar' meant. She thought it meant the colour of a bar of chocolate, but she struggled to find the correlation between a bar of chocolate and her father being so angry. Surely, she thought that her father would be pleased to be given bars of chocolate which was hardly in large supply in the Fletcher children's diet.

Wow, Susie thought, *I would have loved to have several colour bars of chocolate.*

The hostility that Susie's parents had experienced in finding accommodation had upset and frightened Susie's parents greatly who had come from the Caribbean to 'The Motherland', by invitation of the UK government, who they felt were now hostile towards them. This state of affairs caused Susie's parents a lot of uncertainty and anguish, with her father doing some soul searching as to whether he had made a huge mistake by coming to the UK, a strange cold land, which had originally welcomed them with open arms to fill their factories and hospitals doing low paid menial jobs, was now turning its back on them.

After numerous unsuccessful attempts to find alternative accommodation, the Fletchers' eventually found another four bedroomed house which was being rented out by an Asian Landlord, who like Susie's parents had come to live in the UK from India seven years before Susie's parent's arrival to the UK; and who like the Fletchers shared a common understanding of the difficulties as immigrants trying to make a life in the UK for himself and his family.

The only downside and proviso to living at the new accommodation and Susie's new home, was that Susie's mother had the unenviable task of collecting the rent on a weekly basis from the other four single male tenants who shared the house with Susie's family, as well as cleaning the entire house from top to bottom. In return the family would live in the house rent free.

There were many occasions where Susie's mother could be heard having heated arguments with some of the tenants who were sometimes behind with their rent. To add insult to injury, Susie's mother would also cook for the other male tenants, who appeared to be taking her kindness for granted.

Susie's mother would say to her father on numerous occasions, "We can't go on living like this any longer. I think we should buy our own house because I'm tired of looking after these lazy men."

However, although the Fletchers had high aspirations to buy their own home, they were far from being in an economically stable position to buy their own home. Mr

Solomon Fletcher was the sole bread winner who worked six days a week, and Mrs Ruby Fletcher a housewife with five small children.

Mr Solomon Fletcher often spoke about the difficulty in getting a loan from the Banks in order to buy a house for his family. This loan would provide an avenue of escape from the uncertainty and instability of renting substandard cold damp, and overcrowded rooms. The Fletcher children's health was impacted by the family's appalling living conditions, which had a detrimental effect on Susie's health. She had been admitted to hospital on numerous occasions with recurrent chest infections and bronchitis.

Mr Solomon Fletcher decided to set up a 'Pardoner' club, in order to raise funds in which to pay for a deposit on buying a house for the family. The Pardoner was similar to a small Banking arrangement, or savings account system but without the charging of interest, whereby around a number of people who were working, paid an agreed amount of money into the pardoner club, when they were paid on a weekly basis. After around ten weeks any of the pardoner members would be able to ask for the whole amount of the pardoner monies saved in order to pay for goods, or to send money to support their families in the Caribbean, or for travels back to the Caribbean to visit their relatives. Once that person had taken their 'draw' as it was also termed, then they would have to go to the back of the queue in order to allow the other pardoner members to have their turn. Mr Solomon Fletcher nominated Mrs Ruby Fletcher to be in charge of this arrangement, to collect the monies from the pardoner members which varied in numbers between five and fifteen. If a pardoner member failed to keep up with their pardoner payments, then they would be banned from being a pardoner member. Mr Solomon Fletcher had recited the story of several pardoner groups that had been disbanded because in Mr Solomon Fletcher's words and Jamaican patois, "Dem did steal di money," meaning that the people who were left in charge of looking after the pardoner money in their safe keeping had stolen the pardoner members hard earned cash. Mr Solomon Fletcher was adamant that he wouldn't allow that situation to happen to himself, and so decided to take control himself. He was not prepared to miss the opportunity to be a homeowner in the not too distance future.

Chapter 5

Church Attendance in the Fletchers' House

Being very devout Evangelical Christians and getting dressed for Sunday morning Service was a very busy occasion in their household, whereby Susie's parents would send Susie and her siblings off to Sunday School, whilst her parents attended the main Church Service later in the morning.

"Come on now!" Her father would shout to Susie and her siblings. "De church van has arrived."

Susie's parents no longer held their Sunday Church services in the family home because they did not want to risk having their tenancy being taken away from them. The Fletchers' new Landlord informed Susie's parents that their tenancy invoked the clause that they would not be permitted to hold church services in the family home, and to keep the noise down to the bare minimum. Otherwise, they would be evicted.

Instead, Sunday Church services took place in a rented large School Hall on a Sunday morning and evening, where Susie her four other siblings and the congregation of forty men women and their children. Here, they were able to sing pray and stamp their feet to their hearts delight as part of their worship. With one proviso, the school Care-Taker instructed that the congregation pay their rent on time and to keep the school hall clean and tidy.

Chapter 6
Local Authority Care Looms for the Fletcher Children

Susie in particular became a handful to look after and became very clingy to her mother when Mrs Ruby Fletcher broke the news that she was expecting her sixth child. Susie was like Mrs Ruby Fletcher's shadow and would follow her mother everywhere that she went, much to the frustration of her mother. Mrs Ruby Fletcher expressed to Mr Solomon Fletcher that she was finding it very difficult to care for Susie and her siblings due to suffering from a very difficult pregnancy. Mr Solomon Fletcher was working long hours and coming home late at night and was not available to assist Mrs Ruby Fletcher with the children. The Fletchers had no extended family in Northampton in which to support them with their expanding brood. Mr Solomon Fletcher arranged for Susie and four siblings to be looked after by a childminder Mrs Greenwood who lived in the local neighbourhood, in order to give Mrs Ruby Fletcher some respite three times a week in the mornings.

Susie found it very difficult to settle when she was taken with her siblings to Mrs Greenwood the Child Minder's house. Susie would often cry when her mother left her in the care of the Child-Minder. Mrs Greenwood eventually plucked up the courage to tell Susie's mother that she could no longer care for Susie because she had become such a handful by her persistent crying and being generally unsettled. Susie's siblings on the other hand, took to Mrs Greenwood like a 'duck to water'.

Chapter 7

The Fletcher Children are Taken into Local Authority Care

As a result of Susie's mother experiencing major difficulties in her sixth pregnancy, she was taken into Local Authority care in Northampton along with her siblings because their mother had been admitted into hospital. Mr Solomon Fletcher being the family's main bread winner was unable to take time off from work to care for the Fletcher children. Susie was confused and bewildered by the fact that she had been separated from her mother and placed in a strange place where the children looked like adults and seemed so tall, compared to a very thin four-year-old like herself. Her older brother, Freddie, seemed to have settled well into their new 'home', and appeared to take everything in his stride.

Susie was taken into a large room on the first day that they were taken into care. The room was filled with children much older than Susie and her siblings. She also noticed that the children looked very different to them. The room fell silent when they were taken into the room. The children towered over the Fletcher children, who stared at them giving off a very cold atmosphere in their demeanour. Susie had no recollections of being introduced to the group of older children, nor did she remember being spoken to kindly, hugged, cuddled or consoled by the female staff at the home when she became very distressed and frightened by her strange surroundings. There was a large television that had been placed onto a tall cabinet in the middle of the room which had the volume turned up very loudly. The horse racing was on the television with the frantic male sport journalist commentating on the race that was taking place. Susie was lifted onto the cabinet next to the large television. What took place next would change her view of the UK forever.

A large woman came up to Susie and proceeded to cut off all her hair with a large pair of scissors. She started to cry protesting very loudly at the top of her voice and screaming the words 'Mammie! No!' very loudly, and hysterically, to no avail, trying to cover her head with her hands as the large woman pressed her large buxom chest over her very small frame chopping at her thick long locks in a rhythmical fashion, her ears deafened to her cries of protest to stop and for her 'Mammie' to rescue her from what seemed like a bad nightmare that seemed to go on forever, and ever, which she thought that she would eventually awaken from. But this was not to be. It was in fact, 'living a nightmare in reality' and there was nothing that Susie could do to stop this assault on her hair which left her head pulsating with pain and dizziness leaving her head and body feeling very cold. Susie was in a state of shock and confusion. Her long thick hair that her mother had lovingly combed and plaited ritually on a daily basis had been lost forever and had been reduced to a pile of thick black fluff on the floor. Susie was reduced to the appearance of a little boy. Her frilly dresses, ankle socks and sandals were replaced with red jumper and red/yellow striped trousers. She looked strikingly similar in appearance to Rupert the Bear. At this stage Susie felt as though all her identity had been taken away from her. Susie sobbed and sobbed uncontrollably and clung to her older brother who was also distressed by having witnessed what had happened to his little sister.

The three months that Susie and her siblings spent in Local Authority Care seemed like a lifetime. She was physically assaulted and bullied by the older children in the home on numerous occasions although she could only remember just a few. This may have been Susie's brain acting like a sieve with small holes, retaining the bad memories that were too traumatic to forget. Either way, Susie entered the children's home a happy little girl of four years old and left the home a frightened little girl distrustful of strangers as a result of her bad experiences whilst in the home.

Susie often played in the playroom with her siblings. On one particular afternoon, one of the older and taller girls in the home aged around twelve years, walked over to Susie in the playroom, grabbed her by the scruff of the neck and banged her head against the wall. Susie yelled out screaming loudly as much as her small lungs would allow her, which alerted her siblings to her aid, who had been playing with their toys on the other side of the room. She blurted out in between sobs and holding the side of her head with her right hand,

"My head hurts," – sobbed Susie as she pointed to the tall white girl – "she banged my head on the wall."

One of the female members of staff called Aunty Margaret, came running into the playroom to find out what all the commotion was about.

"What's going on?" She shouted.

The older girl replied, "Susie was running around in the playroom and banged her head on the wall."

"No, I didn't!" Shouted Susie. "You did it!" Shouted Susie as she pointed at the tall white girl.

"Now, now," said Aunty Margaret. "Let me take you to the sick room to get you cleaned up and calmed down."

Susie was led sobbing uncontrollably by Aunty Margaret to the sick room. Susie's forehead had started to protrude to that of a small egg on the right side of her head. Aunty Margaret bathed her forehead with a cold flannel, pressing in places as she exerted pressure, which she said would reduce the swelling.

"You should be more careful Susie and look where you're going when running around in the playroom."

"That big girl pushed me and banged my head on the wall in the playroom," retorted Susie.

Aunty Margaret took no notice to what Susie was saying and hummed an indistinct tune as she continued bathing Susie's forehead.

Chapter 8

Susie is Sent to Bed Early for 'Disobedience'

It was summertime when Susie was taken into care which meant that most of the afternoons were spent in the Children's Home's large sprawling garden, which was littered with swings, slides and scooters. Susie did not have any toys in which to play with at home, and so was in awe of the large garden which was adorned with apple trees, flowers and the variety of toys that she could play with her siblings. She loved the scooter and would ride off at speed on the scooter down the long garden path. Aunty Margaret warned Susie not to scooter past a line in the garden. After several warnings, Susie was sent to bed early in the afternoon, without any tea nor supper for 'disobedience' in not heeding the warnings given by Aunty Margaret.

On entering the large dormitory which was split into two sections for the younger and older girls in the Children's Home, Susie flung herself into bed and dissolved into floods of tears sobbing, "I miss my Mammie. I hate this place. I want to go home."

Susie didn't feel tired because it was the early afternoon, and it was so bright. Being the defiant child that she was, Susie decided to have a wander around the dormitory into the area where the older girls slept. She had now been in the dormitory for a few hours and began to feel very hungry. Tucked under one of the older girls' pillow, she found a small brown paper packet filled with brown ribbed sweets that didn't taste like sweets. Susie was so hungry that she ate the packet of sweets and left the empty packet under the pillow.

Later on, in the evening, the older children arrived in their dormitory which was adjacent to Susie's dormitory. Susie overheard one of the older girls complaining very loudly, that someone had eaten all of her Herbal Menthol cough sweets, leaving the empty packet under her pillow. Susie closed her eyes tightly, pretending to be asleep, just in case the older girl walked into her dormitory and found her awake. Susie thought that she definitely didn't want to receive another beating from the older girls when they discover that she was the culprit.

Chapter 9

New Arrivals at Number 80 Bartholomew Street

Susie's parents decided to move with their children to Birmingham from Northampton because Susie's maternal Aunt and Uncle had recently arrived in the UK from the Caribbean with their young family consisting of twin five-year-old daughters. There was a large Caribbean Christian community in Birmingham. Susie's parents thought that the move would be very beneficial for the family's spiritual and social needs. Being a child to immigrant parents in a predominantly white City of Birmingham in the 1960s brought with it an innumerate number of challenges and experiences which was to follow Susie throughout her childhood into adulthood, with the same tensions existing but in a more subtle manner. Susie lived with her parents and five other siblings in a three-bedroom terraced house in a street that slowly became multi-cultural as immigrants from the West Indies and Asia started to come over to the UK in their dribs and drabs, which was synonymous to the children's nursery rhyme 'The Pied Piper', where all the children followed the pied piper through the streets, mesmerised by his hypnotic tune.

Mrs Ruby Fletcher gave birth to her sixth child, a boy named Benjamin, whilst Susie and her other siblings were in Local Authority care. Benjamin was three months old when the family moved to Birmingham. Unlike the other Fletcher children who all weighed under 6lbs at birth, Benjamin was the heaviest of the Fletcher children, weighing in at a healthy 9lbs. Benjamin was a very happy smiley baby with a cool dark brown complexion and big brown eyes that resembled saucers. The visitors who came to welcome the Fletcher family's new arrival would comment on how baby Benjamin resembled his father Mr Solomon Fletcher. Susie didn't take to baby Benjamin at all. She would often try to distract her mother's attention from Benjamin to herself, by telling her mother that she had a persistent stomach-ache whenever Mrs Ruby Fletcher had Benjamin in her arms. Mrs Ruby Fletcher would often become very short tempered with Susie, telling her that Benjamin was a helpless baby who needed her attention.

Susie's siblings on the other hand were ecstatic to have a baby in the house. Kingsley and Freddie in particular would squabble about which rung on their cramped three-rung bunk bed baby Benjamin would sleep on once he was old enough to come out of the cot which was in their parents' bedroom. Carlton, being the youngest boy slept on the bottom bunk, with Kingsley at the top and Freddie occupied the middle bunk. Mrs Ruby Fletcher would often overhear Kingsley and Freddie squabbling, and she would tell them in no uncertain terms that it would not be safe for Benjamin to share a bed with Kingsley nor Freddie but would instead be sharing a bed with Carlton at the bottom rung when he reached two years old.

Chapter 10

Susie Starts School

Susie had just turned four and a half years old when she started School at her local St Augustine's Nursery in Birmingham. She was very excited to be going to 'Big School', she would recite to her mother Mrs Ruby Fletcher, when her mother asked her what school, she would be going to in a few days' time. Mrs Ruby Fletcher had started to prepare Susie for 'Big School', as her mother would on occasions remind her. She was the first girl in the Fletcher household in the UK to attend an English School. Susie's older brother Kingsley was aged twelve years and was much older than the rest of the Fletcher children. Kingsley was born in Jamaica and had already started attending the 'Special School', for children in Birmingham, where English was their second language.

Susie's eldest brother Kingsley had recently arrived from Jamaica to join the rest of the family in Northampton. She vividly remembered her eldest brother having a thick Jamaican accent which Susie's mother tried very hard to tame. "Yes Auntie!" Kingsley would say to his mother when she had called him from upstairs to help out with the family chores. Kingsley had been living in the UK for three months and still referred to his mother as 'Auntie', and not' Mammie', as the other Fletcher children were all told to call their mother by Mr Solomon Fletcher from a very early age. Susie's mother told Mr Solomon Fletcher that Kingsley was the victim of derision and ridicule from their neighbours Mr and Mrs Clarke. She had to keep Kingsley indoors on many occasions in order to stop them poking fun at him whenever he spoke to them.

Mrs Ruby Fletcher hoped that Kingsley's attendance at the Special School would improve his English-speaking skills and reduce the constant ridicule that Kingsley had to endure, much to the annoyance of Mrs Ruby Fletcher.

However, all focus was now placed on Susie by Mrs Ruby Fletcher because she was very clingy to her mother, which had become even more so as a result of the violent traumatic experiences that she had experienced when she spent a short spell in the Children's Home in Northampton, when Mrs Ruby Fletcher had been taken into hospital to have her sixth child. Mrs Ruby Fletcher had noticed that she had become clingier when she came home with the family's new baby brother Benjamin. Mrs Ruby Fletcher had mentioned to Mr Solomon Fletcher that they needed to keep an eye on her because she had noticed that she couldn't venture out of her sight without Susie crying or putting on her coat if she felt that Mrs Ruby Fletcher was leaving the house to go out shopping at the local Market.

"I can't turn without Susie clinging to my dress!" Mrs Ruby Fletcher would often exclaim to Mr Solomon Fletcher.

"Putting Susie into Local Authority Care has had a detrimental effect on her more than her other siblings, who have all flourished in leaps and bounds."

"She has regressed and I'm very worried that if we don't try to prepare her for Nursery School, she won't be able to cope with the many challenges that may come her way in life. God knows what happened to Susie whilst she was in the Children's Home for three months."

Mr Solomon Fletcher was a man of a few words and replied in his usual deep baritone voice,

"You worry too much, Sister Ruby. Susie is just four years old and will grow out of it."

That was the last conversation that Mrs Ruby Fletcher shared with Mr Solomon Fletcher about her concerns about Susie or any of her other children. It was obvious that Mr Solomon Fletcher did not have a deep understanding of his children, nor did he try to because his shift work at the Steel works in Northampton had taken him away from the family home for long twelve-hour shifts, and when he was at home, he was too tired to help Mrs Ruby Fletcher with the children, apart from disciplining them when the need arose. Mrs Ruby Fletcher's way of preparing Susie for 'Big School', was in the form of bribery, telling Susie that if she was able to go to 'Big School', Mrs Ruby Fletcher would buy Susie a large white paper bag of 'Dolly Mixtures' (from the local Market), which was Susie's favourite sweets.

The Dolly mixtures came in various colours and varieties of shapes and sizes. There was striped, pink cream and white miniature oblong shaped ones, chewy round sugar-coated mixtures, others were round bright pink with a soft chewy centre, with an array of red, blue, green, orange, deep purple and black jelly babies made in the shape of a baby.

Susie was in her element! She particularly liked the bright chewy ones and the round bright pink Dolly Mixture with the soft chewy centre.

Mrs Ruby Fletcher certainly knew how to 'bribe' her 'little shadow' into doing what she wanted her to do whenever Susie became very head strong in getting her own way.

However, as the day approached for Susie to start school, Mrs Ruby Fletcher noticed that Susie started to show signs of anxiety which presented itself in the form of her becoming more clingy than usual, making Mrs Ruby Fletcher's daily routine to care for her baby brother Benjamin and her other siblings almost impossible.

"Mammie! Mammie," Susie would wail holding onto her mother's skirt as Mrs Ruby Fletcher struggled to feed her baby brother Benjamin with his bottled milk, mixed with a yellowy corn meal, which had a slightly thick consistency.

"Susie!" Mrs Ruby Fletcher shouted in exasperation.

"Let go of the hem of my skirt. I'm not going anywhere."

"How can I look after baby Benjamin with you clinging to me like that?"

Susie's screams became louder which resulted in her baby brother Benjamin crying frantically.

"Your loud screaming has caused your baby brother to become distressed!" Mrs Ruby Fletcher exclaimed in a loud voice.

"Your baby brother won't grow if he's not able to have his bottle. You're not the only child who needs my attention," explained Mrs Ruby Fletcher in a purposely lowered tone of voice, as she tried to comfort baby Benjamin by rocking him back and forth. Baby Benjamin was by now screaming at the top of his voice, his arms and legs flailing and shaking in distress.

"I don't want to go to school!" Screamed Susie at the top of her voice, as she stamped her feet defiantly on the stone kitchen floor. Susie's face was awash with tears giving the appearance as though she had placed her face under a full running tap.

"I want to stay at home with Mammie!"

By now Susie's regular tantrums had caught the attention of her other siblings who had gathered at the entrance of the door to the kitchen and the outside door that led to the Fletchers' very small back garden (where they had been playing).

Susie was initially oblivious to her sibling's arrival and presence at the entrance to the kitchen and continued wailing and stamping her feet. Susie's tantrum was brought to an abrupt end when her siblings started to mimic her actions.

Mrs Ruby Fletcher's day would start at five in the morning when she would arise to prepare Mr Solomon Fletcher's breakfast which would consist of two raw eggs whisked into a large cup, boiled oats porridge and a large enamel mug of tea.

Chapter 11

Chastisement in the Fletcher Family

Mr Solomon Fletcher, like countless Afro-Caribbean Fathers who came from Jamaica to settle in the UK in the 1950s for economic reasons, had suffered a hard life 'back home' in Jamaica, and was often over heard by Susie, by her father's conversations in the front room (which was where her parents would entertain friends and visitors) where 'big people conversations', took place, as Mr Solomon Fletcher would call it, meaning that Susie and her siblings were never allowed to be privy to the conversations between her parents and the visitors who would come over to the Fletcher family home on a Saturday evening.

Mr Solomon Fletcher and his visitors would recall the very difficult living conditions that they had endured in Jamaica. His own home life was no different and was very dysfunctional. His own Father had ten children with his mother, and several other children with multiple women. His father would flitter to and fro, from the family home. Mr Solomon Fletcher was often left as a young seven-year-old boy with his five older male siblings to take charge of the land so that the family could eat. This was the norm in many of the families across Jamaica. Added to the poverty that blighted many of the Jamaican families was the physical beatings that was named 'discipline', which was meted out mainly by the Jamaican Fathers upon their children and their wives and partners who they thought threatened their authority.

Mr Solomon Fletcher would share his difficult life experiences in Jamaica with his male visitor Mr Samuels, "I never went to school until I was 15 years old because I had to help my father in the field, along with my older brothers with the rearing of goats, chickens, donkeys and the planting of vegetables, sugar-cane, yams, bread fruits and all manner of root vegetables."

"My old man used to beat all of my brothers, sisters and mother with a guava stick which he cut off from de guava tree. Dat stick really did sting when it hit your body," he said, in between mouthfuls of the juicy guava which he shared with Mr Samuels, with the juices dribbling down his mouth and onto the plastic covering on the three-seater settee in the front room.

The penny then dropped, and Susie then realised where this practice of severe physical chastisement had originated from. Mr Solomon Fletcher ruled his household with a rod of iron and treated any dissent punishable by a beating with a worn-looking dark brown leather belt which Mr Solomon Fletcher had purchased from the local cobblers shop up the road from the family home. The belt's proper usage was to support heavy duty work trousers.

Susie's earliest experiences where she and her siblings were beaten, usually occurred when they were upstairs playing. Mr Solomon Fletcher would shout, "Stop di noise upstairs! Don't let me have to come upstairs and beat you all!"

Invariably, the Fletcher children would be so engrossed in their playing and having fun, that they would not have heard Mr Solomon Fletcher's warning. The next thing that would happen would send all the Fletcher children into a spin with Mr Solomon Fletcher beating all the children indiscriminately as the Fletcher children jumped into a light brown metal clothes container. The Fletcher boys would push their female siblings to the front of the metal tin, whilst they shielded themselves against the fast and furious lashes that Mr Solomon Fletcher would rain down onto his five children, with each lash sending out a loud scream from the Fletcher girls, who took all the painful lashes from the belt because they were at the front and in the firing line. Susie and Ruby, her sibling would scream at the top of their voices in unison, "Yes Daddy, no Daddy, sorry Daddy." Mr Solomon Fletcher would shout at his children whilst actively beating them, "Me did warn you to stop the ramping upstairs," Mr Solomon Fletcher would shout. The word 'ramping' was the word that Mr Solomon Fletcher used to mean 'playing'.

The beating would go on for what seemed a life time. Mr Solomon Fletcher only stopped the rapid and relentless beating due to the sweat trickling down from his forehead onto his face causing his eyes to close, thus restricting his vision. Mr Solomon Fletcher would then instruct all his children to find a book to read and go downstairs where he could keep an eye on all the children who by now were all crying profusely. Mr Solomon Fletcher would shout, "Stop di crying. I will give you something to cry about."

As Susie made her way down the winding bare stairs and into the living room, and still crying profusely, she sobbed, "My arms and back hurt. Look at the wails on my arms!"

Susie's siblings gathered around her as she showed them the thick raised raging looking bruises that had criss-crossed across her back and arms, where her father Mr Solomon Fletcher had rained down with brutal force the strikes from the worn-looking dark brown belt which had caused her fragile slender frame to shake with pain and shock. "It really stings," sobbed Susie, who was dressed in a cotton pink and white sleeveless floral dress. Susie suddenly stopped in mid flow of her conversation with her siblings and tried desperately to swallow her tears because she had heard her father Mr Solomon Fletcher enter the living room. Her other siblings quickly left Susie's side and scattered grabbing their reading books which they had thrown carelessly onto the floor in the living rom.

"I don't want to hear another word from any of you today. Do you hear me?" Mr Solomon Fletcher told the Fletcher children. "Yes, Daddy," replied the Fletcher children in unison. For the rest of the day, one could hear a pin drop due to Mr Solomon Fletcher forbidding any of his children from saying a word to each other. Ruby wrapped her arms lovingly around her older sister Susie's neck, with her thumb stuck firmly in her mouth, with the sound of sucking being the only sound that broke the uncomfortable silence that had descended upon the Fletcher household.

The Fletcher children appeared to have short memories when it came to being chastised for trivial 'misdemeanours' such as playing in the house. The next occasion out of many when Mr Solomon Fletcher would mete out physical chastisement on his children, occurred when Susie was trying to enter her brother's bedroom. Again, it was a Saturday afternoon, which seemed like a coincidence when one of the

Fletcher children, namely Susie would get beaten for doing, or not doing one thing or another.

There was a taboo in the Fletchers' household whereby it was forbidden for the females in the family from entering the boys' room. Mr Solomon Fletcher was very much a chauvinistic man who had very strong ideas about 'men' and 'women' roles. He was not very different to men of his generation and also of many Jamaican men of his era at the time, who saw women's roles as being centred around the home.

Susie being the determined and strong-willed girl that she was, decided to ignore Mr Solomon Fletcher's instruction. "Get out of my bedroom," shouted Carlton as Susie tried to force her way into Freddie's bedroom. "Please let me have four of your marbles Freddie," Susie pleaded, as she tried to force her way into her brother's bedroom. "No. I won't give you any of my marbles because I want to play them with my friends at school," Freddie replied.

Playing with marbles was a very popular game that was being played, mainly by the boys at school. The marbles came in a variety of colours. Susie was the tomboy in the family, being surrounded by three brothers. She wouldn't take the word 'no' for an answer.

Susie barged her way into her brother's bedroom by pushing her back against the door.

Mr Solomon Fletcher heard the commotion that was occurring upstairs between Susie and Freddie. He didn't have time to fetch the belt which had been placed on the kitchen table during breakfast time in the morning, as a reminder to the Fletcher children by their father in order to keep them 'in their place and under heavy manners', Mr Solomon Fletcher would warn them.

Mr Solomon Fletcher had the tendency to run up the stairs stealthily which would on most occasions catch the Fletcher children by surprise.

"What did I tell you Susie?" Mr Solomon Fletcher asked Susie in a stern voice. "Not to go into the boys' room, Daddy," replied Susie with her eyes staring down at the bare wooden floor, in order to avoid eye contact with her father's scowling angry face. Susie slowly looked up at her father and noticed that Mr Solomon Fletcher was not carrying the dark brown leather belt in which to beat her with and thought that she had got away with not having a beating for disobeying her father's instructions. However, how wrong Susie was to believe that she wouldn't be beaten.

Mr Solomon Fletcher usually wore a brown checked shirt with braces and a black belt around his waist in which to hold his large black trousers up with. As Susie lifted up her head to look at her father, he reached for his belt unfastened it from the buckle and pulled the belt from across his waist striking Susie's left eye with the buckle of the belt. Susie yelped out in severe pain and shock, her small fragile frame shaking in extreme pain from the impact from the buckle of the belt which had caught her unawares. "Aargh, aargh, aargh!" Susie screamed, holding her left eye with both hands and almost falling backwards onto her brother Freddie. "I can't see!" Her father Mr Solomon Fletcher stood back in shock and stopped beating Susie. "Oh Lord," said Mr Solomon Fletcher. "I caught you with the buckle end of di belt. I pulled the belt out of my trousers di wrong way." Mr Solomon Fletcher lead the screaming Susie into his bedroom which was up another flight of stairs from her brother's bedroom. Susie's left eye by this time had suddenly swelled so much with a large red raging boil which had by now closed her left eye.

Mr Solomon Fletcher opened his dark oak wardrobe and took out a bottle of White Bay Rum to bath Susie's left eye. "Ow! Ow! Ow! Ow!" screamed Susie as Mr Solomon Fletcher bathed her left eye with the white rum which felt as though it was burning a hole into her eye. Susie was inconsolable, crying continuously with muffled indistinct words in between.

After Susie had stopped crying and was sitting in the living room with her other siblings watching their favourite television programme, 'Thunder Birds'. Mr Solomon Fletcher instructed Susie, "If the teacher ask you what happened to your eye when you go to school, you should tell them that you fell off the wall. Okay!"

"Yes, Daddy," replied Susie apprehensively.

Mr Solomon Fletcher walked into the kitchen where Mrs Ruby Fletcher was cooking the family's evening meal, leaving the door ajar, so that Susie was able to eavesdrop on her parent's conversation.

"I struck Susie with di buckle, di wrong end of the belt," Mr Solomon Fletcher told Mrs Ruby Fletcher.

"I did tell you that you're beating the children too much!" Exclaimed Mrs Ruby Fletcher.

Mrs Ruby Fletcher went onto to say, "Remember last week our next-door neighbour Mrs Brown threatened to call the authorities because she said that she could hear the children screaming and crying in the house almost every day of the week?" Mrs Brown, the Fletchers' next neighbour was referred to by Mr Solomon Fletcher as a 'busy body', because she would regularly knock on the wall and would often come around to the front door out of concern for the children's welfare whenever she heard Mr Solomon Fletcher's loud baritone voice whilst he was beating the children, brought on as a result of the loud screaming and crying by the children.

There was a Jamaican Welfare Officer by the name of Mr Elroy, who had become a regular visitor to the Fletchers' home. Susie was unsure as to how he had become involved with the family because whenever Mr Elroy would visit the family home, he would be ushered into the front room as though under an air of secrecy, whereby all the Fletcher children would then be told sternly by Mr Solomon Fletcher to go up to their rooms for the rest of the evening. Susie thought that probably Mr Elroy was visiting her parents in order to ascertain how her oldest brother was settling into the UK because he had recently arrived from Jamaica and had problems assimilating into school life which was very different to the schools in Jamaica.

"You're not in Jamaica now Brother Fletcher where children are beaten over there with no questions asked by anyone," retorted Mrs Ruby Fletcher.

"There are Laws in this country. If we're caught hitting our children in the UK we can get sent to prison, and our children could be taken off us and taken into care by the authorities forever. We don't want that to happen," said Mrs Ruby Fletcher.

"Me know dat, Sister Ruby," retorted Mr Solomon Fletcher.

"We need to keep Susie off school next week because if she goes to school with her left eye in the bruised condition that it is on Monday, the teachers will question her about how she got the bruising to her eye."

The beatings of the Fletcher children by Mr Solomon Fletcher were not only confined to the family home. Mr and Mrs Ruby Fletcher would take their six children to the local evangelical church which was held in a school hall. In order to keep his children in line, Mr Solomon Fletcher would carry the belt as a form of deterrent to bad behaviour, which he would place in the brown rugged looking large leather briefcase which he used, to carry his church song books and Bible. Mr Solomon Fletcher would always point to his briefcase whilst in church to warn his offspring what was in store for them should they misbehave whilst the church service was in full swing. It was usually Susie's brothers who were regularly taken out of the church services and beaten in the dark corridors of the school hall building, their screams invariably drowned out by the loud singing, the knocking of tambourines, clapping and stamping of the congregation's feet on the concrete floor.

Chapter 12

When the Dark Cloud Descended Upon the Fletchers' Household

Susie would often reflect on life changing traumatic experiences that took place in the Fletcher house. Mr Solomon Fletcher was a very domineering man who controlled the purse strings in the Fletcher home. Mrs Ruby Fletcher was given a meagre allowance on a Friday in which to feed and clothe her six children. Mrs Ruby Fletcher's role was to stay at home as a housewife to look after the children whilst Susie's father went out to work. Mr Solomon Fletcher also controlled what clothes Mrs Ruby Fletcher wore and would often take Mrs Ruby Fletcher out shopping to buy clothes that he chose that she would wear to church services. Mrs Ruby Fletcher would often comment to Mr Solomon Fletcher that she didn't like green when he had bought her a light green dress, which made her look like a diseased 'Dutch elm' tree.

Susie couldn't recall the moment when her father started beating her mother. In her mind, Susie thought that all men beat their wives, which Susie thought that was the norm. The earliest recollection where Susie saw Mr Solomon Fletcher hit her mother occurred one late Saturday evening when all the family were seated around the kitchen table, having a late dinner. The kitchen fire was crackling away in the dimly lit kitchen. Mrs Ruby Fletcher was humming away as she scraped away at the burnt-crusted rice in the large enamel pot. Mr Solomon Fletcher was seated around the table, when he suddenly jumped up from the table and grabbed Mrs Ruby Fletcher around the throat pulling her towards the open kitchen fire, pushing Mrs Ruby Fletcher's bottom towards the open flames. The Fletcher children were in shock and stopped eating their rice and peas; Jamaican traditional meal, their mouths ajar speechless in shock and horror. Mrs Ruby Fletcher screamed,

"Brother Fletcher, I didn't waste the shopping money that you gave me!" She shouted in between breaths. "It's not easy feeding six children on the meagre money that you give me on a Friday afternoon!" Mr Solomon Fletcher was a man of few words who would use physical violence in order to get Mrs Ruby Fletcher and all the children in the family to adhere to his instructions. Mr Solomon Fletcher expected Mrs Ruby Fletcher to be very frugal whenever she went shopping and held a tight reign of the family's purse strings. Mrs Ruby Fletcher would obtain credit from various Asian shops in order clothe her growing brood and would often hide the clothes that she had purchased at the bottom of her wardrobe underneath layers of blankets and sheets.

Mr Solomon Fletcher's violent treatment towards his family had created an atmosphere within the Fletcher family where his children and wife Mrs Ruby Fletcher were all in fear of him, except for Susie, who resented her father profusely, and was determined that she wouldn't allow herself to be frightened by someone whose only way to get control and servitude by his family was to beat them senseless until they relented to his request. Susie saw Mr Solomon Fletcher's outward persona of an upright hard-working Christian man as a façade to the reality of a fierce dominating man who ruled his family with 'a rod of iron', which was a replica of his own brutal upbringing in Jamaica. This conflict in cultural differences in the discipline of the Fletcher children and the unequal treatment towards his wife, shone a bright light on the constant internal war that was going on within Mr Solomon Fletcher's conscience and soul, who was not living the 'proper Christian life' in the family home, (that was the religious requirement by the Evangelical Christians) by being a shining example to his wife and children. Instead, Mr Solomon Fletcher's violent outbursts was the contrary, that would shatter those ideals, which would in reality get the better of him.

Mr Solomon Fletcher replied to Mrs Ruby Fletcher in his loud and angry baritone voice,

"Me did tell you to not to spend all di money at once!"

Mr Solomon Fletcher continued to push Mrs Ruby Fletcher's bottom closer towards the open fire when Susie jumped up from the kitchen table. Running towards her father like a 'red rag to a bull'.

"Leave Mammie alone!" Susie shouted at the top of her voice as she tugged ferociously like a wild animal at her father's blue and cream patterned jumper. Susie's other siblings were at this stage all crying loudly in unison.

Mr Solomon Fletcher was taken aback by Susie's persistence and released his grip on Mrs Ruby Fletcher who by now was crying, and who told Mr Solomon Fletcher in between her sobs, "I'm going to fast and pray for you!"

Mrs Ruby Fletcher was a very devout Christian who would fast and pray on various days in the month about family issues that were on her mind and of great concern and needed resolving. Mrs Ruby Fletcher's faith in God was very strong and she believed that God could change Mr Solomon Fletcher's violent outbursts towards his family.

Susie had over the years begun to resent her father for the endless occasions and times that he had physically disciplined her, her siblings and her mother for trivial misdemeanours that her father had said that they had been guilty of.

Susie had learned a song at School which she would regularly sing when Mr Solomon Fletcher would beat her mother in her parent's bedroom late into the night whilst the children would be snugly tucked up in bed and asleep, except for Susie, who would hear every smack and thump accompanied by Mrs Ruby Fletcher's shrieks of pain at each beating.

Susie felt desperately afraid for her mother, as she had always been, whenever the summertime approached every year because she knew that Mrs Ruby Fletcher was going to be in for a 'rough ride', whereby her father would be beating her mother relentlessly during the late summer nights. Susie had overheard Mrs Ruby Fletcher telling her father she knew when he would be beating her because on the nights of the beatings, he would refrain from praying.

These beatings would then peak in the late summertime for some unknown reason when Mr Solomon Fletcher's beatings on Susie's mother would be at its most severe and dangerous. Susie would often recite the chorus of the song that she had learned at school in mantra fashion whilst sitting on her bed.

The chorus of the song went along the lines,

"Oh! Susanna, do not cry for me; I come from Alabama, with my Banjo on my knee."

Susie would sing this chorus over and over again whilst listening to her mother's moans and stifled cries, which sounded as though Mr Solomon Fletcher had placed something over Mrs Ruby Fletcher's mouth to prevent her screams from waking up the sleeping Fletcher children. There were also noises of loud banging and whipping which Susie thought sounded like a belt being used in a ferocious manner onto Mrs Ruby Fletcher's body. Susie could hear her heartbeat thudding away on her pillow like a high-speed train racing along a long and winding train track, as she clung to her pillow whilst sitting upright in the blackened bedroom. Susie listened to her sister Ruby's snoring who was fast asleep and 'away with the fairies', oblivious to the drama that was unfolding in the Fletcher home. Susie was relieved that Ruby was asleep and wouldn't have to hear and endure further bad memories of her father's physical assault on their mother. Susie sat on the top of her bedcovers for what seemed like eternity. She had a plan. She would alight from her bed and go up a flight of stairs along the long corridor to her parent's bedroom, where she would bang on her parent's bedroom door, (as she had done dozens of times in order to rescue her screaming mother who sounded to be in a lot of distress) to inform her mother that she needed to use the outside toilet. Susie shouted whilst banging on her parent's door,

"Mammie! Mammie! Mammie!" – Susie shouted sobbing profusely – "I want to use the outside toilet."

"Go back to your bed!" Shouted Mr Solomon Fletcher. "It's late."

"But I want to go to the toilet," insisted Susie as she sobbed, determined to get her mother's attention to come out of her parent's bedroom and out onto the landing. Susie was really worried about the state in which she would find her mother in.

On the numerous other occasions when Mrs Ruby Fletcher had suffered a beating from Mr Solomon Fletcher, she would bear the scars of a swollen face, in particular her cheekbones looked raised and 'angry' from the punches that had been delivered by Mr Solomon Fletcher onto her face, and bruised arms which Susie saw from her mother's short sleeved night dress.

"Are you alright, Mammie?" Sobbed Susie as her mother gingerly walked out of the bedroom, wearing a long light blue dressing gown.

"I'm alright, Susie," replied her mother, as she tried without success to rein in her dishevelled hair.

"Come on. I will take you to the toilet," continued Mrs Ruby Fletcher, with reddened eyes and her voice cracking in places as she spoke.

Mr Solomon Fletcher stood halfway inside the bedroom, his tall broad frame towering over Mrs Ruby Fletcher and Susie. Susie looked up into Mr Solomon Fletcher's face giving him a scowling look as she did so.

"And go straight back to your bedroom when you've come back from the toilet. You should be sleeping in your bedroom," retorted her father.

Mrs Ruby Fletcher would lead Susie sobbing down the endless flights of cold wooden stairs, through the living room and through the kitchen, to the toilet outside, with Susie clutching tightly onto her mother's hand.

As on many occasions after Susie had 'rescued' her mother from the cruel clutches of her violent and abusive father, Mrs Ruby Fletcher would spend the rest of the night in Susie and Ruby's bedroom, snuggling up and between Susie and Ruby in their double bed. Mrs Ruby Fletcher would push the large old dark brown wooden wardrobe next to the door in order to prevent Mr Solomon Fletcher from gaining entry into the bedroom during the night. Susie, however, would never settle after such traumatic events, and would stay awake for the remainder of the night, like a 'watchman', just in case her father tried to gain entry into the bedroom. However, there were a few times when Mr Solomon Fletcher would knock on the bedroom door imploring Mrs Ruby Fletcher to come back to their bedroom. Mrs Ruby Fletcher would succumb to Mr Solomon Fletcher's plea and return to the bedroom. Susie would not be able to fall asleep fearing that her mother would be in danger, listening to every creak that the large house would make.

Susie remembered vividly as though it was yesterday when her father's violent outburst took a further sinister turn. Once again it was mid-summer nearing the end of July, when Mr Solomon Fletcher's violent outbursts erupted whilst the Fletcher children were snuggled up in bed and fast asleep. Susie was awake, as she was during the numerous occasions when her father would upset the tranquillity of the peaceful and sleepy family home. Susie bolted upright in her bed as she heard the distinct ears piercing painful shrieks of her mother descending from her parents' bedroom onto the landing below and into Susie and Ruby's bedroom. Susie's heart started to thump very quickly against her pillow as she pressed the pillow firmly against her chest, her lower lip quivering with fear and in trepidation at the sudden loud noises and commotion that was coming from her parents' bedroom. The room was pitch black with the dark green heavy 'water baby' curtains that blocked out the chinks of light into the dark bedroom. Susie could hear her younger sister Ruby sleeping contentedly sucking away at her thumb in the double bed that they shared together. She started to sing the chorus of the song that she had always sung when this 'dark cloud' descended yet again on the Fletcher family home. Susie would sing,

"Oh Susanna, do not cry for me; I come from Alabama, with my Banjo on my knee."

Susie would often wonder how her three brothers, (barring baby Benjamin) slept throughout so soundly whilst her father 'knocked nine bells' out of their mother on so many countless occasions during the middle of the night. Susie thought that maybe her brother's bodies had become paralysed with shock and fear from the violent sound of Mr Solomon Fletcher beating their mother that they just couldn't move or awake out of their slumber. Susie on the other hand was fearless. She feared for her mother's safety and well-being from her father's beatings but did not fear for her own safety. Susie nudged her sleeping sister Ruby.

"Ruby! Ruby! Ruby!" whispered Susie. "Daddy's beating Mammie! Mammie's crying loudly!"

Ruby started crying at what Susie had told her. "I want Mammie, I want Mammie!" Cried Ruby, with her thumb in her mouth as she clung onto Susie's yellow dress like a baby koala.

"We must go to Mammie's room," Susie told Ruby as she held her hand whilst reaching for the light switch. As Susie and Ruby stepped out into the dark landing, Susie heard Mrs Ruby Fletcher running across the landing down the stairs from her bedroom towards them.

"Come on girls," whispered Mrs Ruby Fletcher. We're leaving this house.

"Are you alright, Mammie?" Susie asked her mother.

Susie noticed that Mrs Ruby Fletcher was wearing a creased white scarf on her head and a brown coat, which revealed parts of her red nighty underneath. Mrs Ruby Fletcher held Susie's pink coat in her hands which she gave to her to put on, and hurriedly assisted Ruby to put on her white coat.

"Where are we going Mammie?" Susie asked her mother, as Mrs Ruby Fletcher held Susie and Ruby's hands as she led them down the dimly lit landing and down the bare wooden stairs and out through the front door, closing the heavy door quietly behind her, so as not to wake the Fletcher boys who were still fast asleep in their beds.

"We're going to Pastor Brown's house," replied Mrs Ruby Fletcher. "Your daddy needs to be prayed for by Pastor Brown and Evangelist Brown."

Pastor Brown and Evangelist Brown were the 'Spiritual Mother and Father' of the local church that Susie and her parents attended. They were the people that members of the church would go to for spiritual guidance, prayer and support in any area of their lives that they felt was causing them concern. Pastor Brown was a short plump light skinned man with a thick bushy moustache whose commanding loud voice made up for his short stature. He always wore an off-white shirt, with a large grey tie that always appeared too tight, where the folds of skin around his neck would drape over his crumpled shirt which resembled a pink blancmange. He was always dressed in an ill-fitting pin striped black and grey suit, black and white striped shoes with thin pointed toes. Susie liked Pastor Brown's wife Evangelist Brown, who was a slim dark-skinned woman, who had a large black mole on the left side of her face next to her mouth. She had a wide smile which revealed shinny white teeth with a gold tooth implant in the middle of her top teeth. She always wore a black hat which covered her short black curly thick hair neatly, which was firmly folded at the back of her head into a black hair net. Evangelist Brown was slightly taller than her husband. She often wore two-piece dresses which were often low cut at the bust with matching short figure-hugging jackets. Evangelist Brown was known to make her own clothes which always complemented her slim figure. She was a kind motherly woman who was loved and respected by the women and mothers in the church.

As Susie and her sister Ruby and mother walked down the dimly lit dark cobbled streets with Mrs Ruby Fletcher, she wondered what effect or difference prayer would have on her father Mr Solomon Fletcher, who seemed intent on dominating the whole family with his regular onslaught of vicious beatings, taking little notice about what the biblical teachings said about loving his wife and 'not provoke his children to wrath'.

The walk to Pastor Brown's house seemed endless and to take forever, making Susie feel dizzy with the narrow winding streets which all looked the same, with not a soul in site, except for the odd grey feral cat that ran out from behind the black dust bin at the side of the street and out across the street where Susie lost sight of it as it became lost in the shadows of the cold night. Ruby started crying complaining to Mrs Ruby Fletcher that she was tired and that she wanted Mrs Ruby Fletcher to pick her up because her legs were tired.

"We're nearly there, Ruby." Mrs Ruby Fletcher explained to Ruby.

Mrs Ruby Fletcher finally arrived at Pastor Brown's house which had the same external appearance as the Fletchers' home. Mrs Ruby Fletcher knocked loudly at the door, shouting as she did so, "Pastor Brown! Evangelist Brown," shouted Mrs Ruby Fletcher through the black rusty letter box.

"Who's that?" Shouted a male voice from the upstairs darkened window. Susie recognised the voice to be that of Pastor Brown through the half-opened sash upstairs bedroom window.

"It's Sister Fletcher," replied Mrs Ruby Fletcher. "Brother Fletcher needs prayers," explained Mrs Ruby Fletcher.

"Wait a minute," – explained Pastor Brown – "I will wake Evangelist Brown."

Susie continued looking up at the sash window which was now closed. She saw the dim light coming from the grey patterned curtains and heard the hushed indistinct chatter of Pastor Brown and Evangelist Brown from the front bedroom above.

Pastor Brown opened the front door which exuded a warmth and tranquillity that took Susie by surprise because she had never experienced anything like it before.

"We will come with you back to your house. The children should be asleep in their beds. They shouldn't be walking on the streets at this time of the night. It's two o'clock in the morning," Pastor Brown told Mrs Ruby Fletcher, as he pressed with both hands on his chest, a large black book which had the words 'HOLY BIBLE' written in gold print.

Pastor Brown and his wife escorted Mrs Ruby Fletcher with Ruby in her arms and Susie holding onto the hem of Mrs Ruby Fletcher's brown coat as they walked back home revisiting the winding and dimly lit narrow streets that they had previously travelled.

With Pastor Brown and his wife walking ahead of Susie, Mrs Ruby Fletcher who was struggling to keep up with Pastor Brown and his wife's fast faced walking, due to the heavy weight of carrying Susie's sleeping sister Ruby, Susie was surprised at how quickly and in no time at all that they had arrived back home, compared to the time that it had taken Susie, her mother and her sister Ruby to get to Pastor Brown's house.

Susie felt exhausted, her legs numb from walking and longed for the comfort of her warm bed as they all entered the dimly lit hallway, with Ruby's gentle snoring on her mother's shoulder that broke the eerie silence in the sleepy Fletcher house. Pastor Brown and his wife spared no time in entering the Fletcher house to confront and question Susie's father about what had caused her mother to take two of her six children out of their beds, and out into the cold streets in the early hours of the morning to seek refuge at his house.

Mrs Ruby Fletcher carried Ruby up the wooden stairs, and up into her bedroom with Susie walking sleepily and slowly behind, leaving Pastor Brown and his wife in the hallway.

"I will be down shortly," said Mrs Ruby Fletcher to Pastor Brown and his wife.

As Mrs Ruby Fletcher made her way with Ruby in her arms to Susie and Ruby's bedroom, they were met by Mr

Solomon Fletcher who was in the doorway of Susie and Ruby's bedroom.

Mrs Ruby Fletcher and Susie were startled by Mr Solomon Fletcher's presence.

"Where have you been with Susie and Ruby in de middle of di night?" Mr Solomon Fletcher asked Mrs Ruby Fletcher fiercely in his loud deep baritone voice, unaware of Pastor Brown and Evangelist Brown's presence in the hallway downstairs.

"Keep your voice down," – replied Mrs Ruby Fletcher as she cradled Ruby in her arms – "you will wake Ruby and the rest of the children in the house."

Pastor Brown shouted from the hallway downstairs, which made an echo sound as it reached the landing upstairs, "Brother Fletcher, come downstairs. Me and Evangelist Brown want to have a word with you."

Mr Solomon Fletcher made his way downstairs whilst Mrs Ruby Fletcher settled Ruby back into her bed. Susie was surprised that Ruby had slept throughout the commotion that had taken place between Mr Solomon Fletcher and Susie's mother.

"You must get into your bed too Susie" – whispered Mrs Ruby Fletcher gently – "you won't grow tall if you don't get enough sleep."

"But I want to stay with you, Mammie," replied Susie in a defiant voice.

"I'm not going anywhere. I'm just going downstairs to talk with Pastor Brown and his wife who want to have a word with your father."

Mrs Ruby Fletcher rushed out of the dark bedroom and made her way down the dimly lit wooden stairway and into the hallway at the front of the house, leaving Susie sitting on the top of the sheet covers. Susie refused to give in to the sleep that was descending upon her and started to make her way out of her darkened bedroom and onto the dimly lit landing. Through the gaps in the brown wooden-banister, Susie strained her ears to decipher words from the hushed conversation between Pastor Brown and her parents.

"You must love your wife Sister Fletcher and take care of your family." Susie heard Pastor Brown telling her father, "God's not pleased that you're beating your wife and children."

"When I entered this house, I saw a dark cloud hanging over this house. If I and Evangelist Brown didn't come over tonight, something terrible would have happened to Sister Fletcher."

On hearing what Pastor Brown had told her father, Susie who was deeply troubled by Pastor Brown's revelation, made her way back upstairs into her darkened bedroom, slipping under the sheet next to her sister Ruby who was snoring loudly.

Chapter 13

Mrs Ruby Fletcher and Her Children

The Fletcher children, who had recently arrived in Birmingham had started at St Augustine's School during the third summer term, were looking forward to spending the summer holidays at home with their mother Mrs Ruby Fletcher, who would spoil the Fletcher children rotten by allowing them to have a lie-in, and spend the entire morning in bed, whilst their mother cleaned the house from top to bottom singing along to her favourite religious songs that was playing on the family's Gramophone. One of their mother's favourite songs that she would sing over and over again would be, 'I'd rather have Jesus than silver and Gold', sung by Jim Reeves. Mrs Ruby Fletcher would then cook the Fletcher children their favourite breakfast, which was cooked in the family's well-used black 'Dutch-pot', which was a grey flat-bottomed pot used for slow cooking authentic Caribbean dishes such as soups and casseroles, including the Fletcher family's main Sunday main meal consisting of rice and peas and chicken, which was traditionally eaten in all the Caribbean households in the UK. The smell of their mother's cooking would make its way up the winding stairway and into Susie's bedroom which she shared with her sister Ruby, which would have a bewitching, hypnotic and transforming effect on her dreams. Susie was taken to a magical place where she saw herself sitting around a large dark brown oak table with her siblings and her mother, at the centre of the kitchen plating up fried dumplings, fried sausages, bacon, beans and fried bread dipped in Lard, whilst her siblings covered their own dishes with their hands from each other, fearing that either siblings would take a sausage or two from the other when either of them took their eyes off their food. Susie noticed something very significant in her dream. She noticed that her father Mr Solomon Fletcher was nowhere to be seen. *Had he gone to work earlier in the morning?* Susie thought. Susie looked around the room in her dream for the rusty brown hook where her father would leave his bottle blue Ruck sack in which he would place has 'packings', as her father would refer to his lunch bag which he carried to work. Instead, in the place of the rusty brown hook was a picture frame which had a photograph, all six of the Fletcher children were smiling and holding hands, with their mother in the middle holding Ruby's hand, with baby Benjamin fast asleep swaddled in a white knitted blanket. Susie then came to the realisation in her deep hypnotic dream that Mr Solomon Fletcher did not live in the family home because there was a different ambience to the atmosphere in the house. However, Susie's young mind could not decipher nor understand why her father did not exist or occupy a space in her dream. Susie was jolted back to reality when she heard her mother shout,

"I've been calling you children for a while now, but nobody is getting up to come downstairs for breakfast. I won't be calling you all again. The time is half past nine and I need to go to the laundrette to wash all the blankets on your beds before your father comes home this evening."

Susie's heart sank because reality had set in, and she realised that she was dreaming after all. She wished that her dream was in fact a reality without her father being present in the family home.

Chapter 14

When the Fletcher Children Were
Left Alone at Home

Life had changed very little for the Fletcher family when they moved from Northampton to Birmingham. Home life for Susie had not improved for the better as her mother Mrs Ruby Fletcher had hoped, but had worsened with her mother taking the brunt of the beatings from Mr Solomon Fletcher, with Susie being the arbitrator sibling of the Fletcher children, who would invariably stand in between her father and mother in order to protect and 'rescue' her mother from her father's Jackal and Hyde monstrous physical grip, which would, unbeknown to Susie, have future dire physical and psychological consequences for her, and putting at risk her place in the Fletcher household.

Due to finances being very tight with an extra mouth to feed, with baby Benjamin's arrival and with the eldest child Kingsley who had recently joined the family into the UK from Jamaica. The Fletcher family was beginning to feel the pinch, and Mrs Ruby Fletcher was reluctantly forced out to work to take on a full-time job working in the local sweatshops in the backstreets of Birmingham, where a small number of mothers from the Black and Asian communities found regular low paid jobs to supplement their husbands' income. It wasn't the 'done thing' for mothers with children in the sixties to go out to work. In fact, it was frowned upon because it was thought that a woman's place was in the home looking after the home and the children. Susie was seven years old when her mother went out to work. It was Mr Solomon Fletcher's unilateral decision that Mrs Ruby Fletcher would need to go out to work in order to help out with the family's finances to keep the family afloat. However, that would mean the three eldest children, namely Kingsley, Freddie and Susie would be left at home alone without an adult present for six long weeks, whilst the younger three children baby Benjamin, Carlton and Ruby would be taken to a well-known Child-Minder in the local community called Sister Wright who lived two streets away from the Fletchers family home.

Susie wasn't impressed with the change of events that she felt had been thrust onto her without her having time to digest her father's unliteral decision for her mother to leave the family home to work full-time. Susie's mind began to imagine all sorts of unexpected catastrophes happening to herself and her two siblings whilst her parents were out at work during the daytime whilst they were at home alone during the long six weeks summer holiday.

This 'bombshell' announcement by her father took Susie back to an incident which occurred one Saturday afternoon when her parents had left her and her siblings, (except baby Benjamin who they took with them) at home alone, in order to attend a Church Business Meeting which her father said was very imperative for himself and their mother to attend, because the Church Leadership had a very important proposition to put to its 80 strong membership which would involve moving out of their rented School hall, where they held their regular Sunday Church Services, to a Church Building which had the capacity to hold around 300 people. However, in order to purchase the Church building would require a financial commitment from its Church membership to pledge to give an agreed amount of money to the Church.

As Susie's parents proceeded to leave Susie and her siblings in the house alone, in order to attend their Church's Business meeting, Mr Solomon Fletcher warned Susie and her siblings that they should not open the front door to strangers if the doorbell rang. Mr Solomon Fletcher told the Fletcher siblings,

"If the doorbell rings you must all lie flat on di the floor and don't move. Do you hear me children?" asked Mr Solomon Fletcher.

"Yes, Daddy," the Fletcher children replied in unison. The Fletcher children knew that any dissent from their father's instructions would have dire consequences.

Susie's parents always dressed in their 'Sunday Best', whenever they attended their local Church, which consisted of Mr Solomon Fletcher dressed in a brown and black pin striped suit, white striped shirt with silver cufflinks, and finished off with black polished shoes. Mrs Ruby Fletcher would wear a bottled green dress with a neatly tied bow at the neckline, covered by a long dark brown coat, with a small black handbag clasped under her right arm. Her mother's black seamed stockings and low black heeled shoes was always a fascination to Susie because unbeknown to her mother, Susie would invariably wear her mother's stockings and shoes whilst at play and pretended to be her mother with her other siblings. Mrs Ruby Fletcher completed her outfit with a purple hat which was perched proudly on her thick mop of curly black hair like an oddly shaped blancmange.

Susie's parents hadn't been away from the family home for very long when the doorbell suddenly rung. Susie had remembered what her father had instructed them to do should the doorbell ring. Susie and her siblings proceeded to dive onto the floor, apart from Freddie her older brother.

Susie's relationship with Freddie had been very close when it was just the two of them living in Northampton where they were born, and Susie had often given Freddie her toy doll to play with whilst she played with his marbles. However, when their older brother Kingsley arrived in the family home from Jamaica, Susie's and Freddie's relationship changed and became strained and distant because Freddie was no longer the eldest in the Fletcher household. Freddie became very critical towards Kingsley's Jamaican accent, and he would invariably make mocking sounds on particular words which Kingsley found very difficult to pronounce, such as the word 'film', which Kingsley would incorrectly pronounce as 'flim'. Freddie would fall about in fits of laughter, to Kingsley's embarrassment, and to Susie's horror at the way that Freddie was treating Kingsley.

"Stop it, stop it" – Susie would scream at the top of her voice – "it's not funny."

Susie would protectively wrap her arms around Kingsley who towered above Susie, like an ill-fitting blanket.

"I'm only joking," Freddie would retort at the top of his voice.

The doorbell carried on ringing incessantly for what seemed like forever to Susie.

"Lie on the floor, Freddie." Susie instructed Freddie.

"Why should I?" Freddie asked cheekily.

"Because Daddy said so," retorted Susie, and mystified by her older brother's defiance.

"I'm not going to," replied Freddie. "I'm going to open the door because it might be my friend Anthony at the door wanting me to come out to play."

Susie replied, "You know that we're not allowed to play out even when Mammie and Daddy are at home."

Freddie ignored his younger sister's protestation and proceeded walking towards the front door. Susie's heart sank as she heard the fast-rhythmic beating of her heart as the doorbell rang, which in some strange way sounded like the beginnings of the orchestral sounds on the Radio 4 programmes, which would ring through the Fletcher family home when their father would be getting ready for work in the early mornings.

"Hello young man," Susie heard a strange voice emanate from the front door. "Is your mother at home?" Susie strained her ears to hear the rest of the conversation between Freddie and the stranger at the door, but she was prevented from doing so, due to the now loud thumping sound coming from the centre of her chest cavity. The conversation between Freddie and the stranger at the door had finished before Susie had the time to say, 'Jack Robinson'.

Susie heard the front door slam loudly. Freddie came bouncing back into the living room where Susie and her other sibling Kingsley was stretched out on the floor.

"You can all get up now!" Freddie shouted. "He's gone now."

"Who was it?" Susie asked impatiently.

"The white man at the door said he was a Bailiff, and that Mammie owes him a lot of money and that he will be taking Mammie to Court," replied Freddie breathing heavily with excitement as he spoke.

"Oh no!" Screamed Susie at the top of her voice and shaking with fear.

"Mammies going to be put in Prison forever and we will never see her again!" Cried Susie, sobbing as she spoke.

She remembered this was not the first time that the Bailiff had visited the Fletcher family home. On numerous occasions the Bailiff had visited their family home asking for Susie's mother when Mrs Ruby Fletcher was at home. Her mother had promised to keep up with her payments, but had fallen behind with her weekly payments, hence the visit by the Bailiff once again.

Susie was the only one who knew a lot about her mother's spending habits. She had been with her mother when she had visited an Asian shop in Birmingham and had bought the Fletcher children's clothes on 'credit', with the shop keeper trusting Susie's mother to pay for the clothes when she could afford to do so. Mrs Ruby Fletcher would disclose to the Asian Shop Keeper that Mr Solomon Fletcher held a very tight rein on the family's finances.

"Don't tell your father, her mother would tell her, as she stuffed the newly bought clothes at the back of Susie's large dark oak wooden wardrobe."

Susie now had visions of her mother being taken to Court by the police and sent to Prison forever. "How would I cope without my mother?" Susie asked herself, trying with enormous difficulty to comprehend what Freddie had just told them.

"We mustn't tell Daddy or Mammie that you opened the front door, or that Mammie owes the Bailiff any money," Susie instructed her siblings. "Do you hear me, Freddie?" Susie shouted.

"Okay, Susie. If I must," replied Freddie reluctantly.

"Anyway, if Daddy found out that you opened the front door to strangers when he told you not to, we will all get a beating," Susie told Freddie.

The incident regarding the visit from the Bailiffs haunted Susie and left an eternal dread in her mind, with the thought that her mother could be taken away from the family home and thrown into prison and never to be seen again, became too much for her to envisage, with Susie vowing to save up all her pocket money that her mother would secretly give to her, in order to give her mother whenever her mother ran out of money. Susie's mind then became settled with the plan that she had devised in order to 'look-out' for her mother as long as she lived.

Chapter 15

Susie Makes Her Mark at St Augustine's School for All the Wrong Reasons

Mrs Ruby Fletcher was very impressed with her 'little shadow', who she thought had turned the corner and had left behind the 'clinging' and 'foot stomping', which Susie who was renowned for over the years when the Fletcher family lived in Northampton. Mrs Ruby Fletcher had proudly mentioned to Mr Solomon Fletcher that Susie was now settling down well in their new home in Birmingham, and that the move from Northampton to the big City of Birmingham had done their children the world of good, especially Susie. Mr Solomon Fletcher being a man of few words was not one to be concerned about his children's well-being and would often say to Susie's mother, invariably in earshot of Susie, "The Bible says that you shouldn't spare di rod and spoil di child. You spoil Susie too much, that's why she gets away with everything. She just needs a good beating and that would stop all di foot stomping and stubbornness."

Susie settled well in the Nursery School and the years passed by rather uneventfully, apart from her first day at St

Augustine's Infant School. Mrs Ruby Fletcher had walked Susie to the School gate and had kissed her goodbye, telling Susie that she would fetch her at Lunch time. Although Susie was apprehensive about moving up from Nursery School into the Infants School, she was reassured by her mother that she would still be with her friends Sheila and Gina who she was very good friends with and had attended their Birthday parties at their homes where she had always won a prize when they played musical chairs.

No sooner had Mrs Ruby Fletcher left Susie in the care of her new teacher Mrs Fitzgerald, that Susie had a sense of foreboding. "Come on now, Susie," said Mrs Fitzgerald. "There shall be no tears coming from you, young lady," she said in a very stern voice.

Mrs Fitzgerald's stature resembled that of a giraffe with a long physique, wearing a pale off-white complexion, with brown spots dotted around her nose and cheeks. Perched onto her nose was a pair of metal-rimmed glasses which gave the impression that it was about to fall off her face. Susie found her new teacher's breath very unbearable as she leaned into Susie's face whilst talking to her in a very demeaning fashion. Mrs Fitzgerald was dressed in a black cream pleated dress with black matching cream sandals which fastened at the back.

Susie joined the rest of the children into the playground. The children were all playing an array of games such 'kiss chase', where the girls chased the boys, whilst the other children played mothers and fathers with their prams and toy dolls. Susie was amazed at the size of the concrete playground which housed St Augustine's Nursery, Infants and Primary, which Susie would be joining. She longed to return to her old

Nursery School. She noticed a pram that was left unattended in the playground and ran quickly across to it before any of the other children would notice it to play with. The leather pram with its black upholstery resembled the one that her mother had used to push the Fletcher children, only that it was miniature in size. The lining on the outside of a detachable hood looked like some type of vinyl with cloth on the inside of the hood. The well-worn metal wheels appeared to have seen better days. Susie hastily jumped into the pram which went hurtling down the playground towards her former Nursey School. The pram was going at such a fast speed that Susie could only cling on for dear life hoping that it would come to a standstill so that she could escape out of the speeding pram. She thought to herself, that it probably wasn't a clever idea to get into the pram after all, whilst it hurtled out of control, heading towards the rose bush that separated St Augustine's Nursery School from her Infant School. As the Pram connected with the rose bush, and before Susie could escape from the pram, she was catapulted into the air and over the rose bush and into St Augustine's Nursery School, falling unceremoniously onto her face loosening both her front teeth. Susie screamed as loudly as her little vocal cords would allow her, with trickles of blood coming from the corners of her mouth onto the concrete playground, where both her top front teeth had hit the ground. Her teachers from the Nursery School ran over to Susie picking her up as one would a rag doll, her thin frame shaking and screaming from the pain and shock that she was feeling.

"Now, now, Susie. What on earth have you been doing!" The teacher exclaimed. "You're a big girl now and shouldn't be lying in a pram. We shall have to get your mother to come and fetch you and take you home. Those two front teeth of yours will need to come out. Now people will think that you have been kissing the boys."

The thought of her kissing the boys repulsed Susie. Indeed, her feelings of foreboding when she was met by her teacher Mrs Fitzgerald earlier at the start of her school day, had indeed manifested itself in less than an hour in school that morning, with Susie having to have both her shaky teeth extracted at her local Dentists. How was Susie going to explain to her friends at her school and to the grown-ups, who she expected would tease her with the words that she had heard being reiterated to her friends at church, 'been kissing the boys again have you?'

Chapter 16

Susie Moves up into St Augustine's Primary School

The tensions were continuing and had increased in intensity in the family home with Mr Solomon Fletcher continuing to dominate the Fletcher children including their mother Mrs Ruby Fletcher which started to have a negative effect on Susie's behaviour at School.

Susie's school life started to change for the worse when she moved up into Primary School. Indeed, her school years at St Augustine's Primary School were far from uneventful.

The boys were now separated from the girls in Primary School which pleased Susie, with having to contend with her annoying brothers at home.

Susie remembered being in awe of St Augustine's Primary School by its imposing tall dark intricate black and grey brickwork, numerous oblong shaped windows with metal trimmings interwoven meticulously, giving the impression that it had once been the residence of the upper classes. The tall chimneys appeared to extend endlessly into the clouds, belching out black soot intermittently like musical instruments in an orchestra, on the different sections of the adjoining school buildings. The low walls around the perimeter of the school were attached to a wiry meshed material which one could look through as one approached the school. The school gate was made out of heavy cast iron material, which Susie's mother had to push forcefully in order to get through the entrance to access the front of the school. This worried Susie somewhat because she had visions of her mother being unable to gain access to the main part of school building at the end of each school day.

Susie looked very smart and grown up in her school uniform, which consisted of a bottled green pleated skirt and pinafore, white shirt, green and black tie, with white knee-high rimmed socks. She wore ill-fitting tight black laced shoes which made a squeaking sound as she walked with her mother through the heavy cast iron school gates and towards the entrance of the school.

The inside of Susie's classroom resembled the outside of the school building, with the exception of its off-white painted brickwork. The classroom had thick white painted column radiators which covered the four corners of the classroom. The heat which emanated from the column radiators gave on ambience of intense warmth and security which Susie had never experienced before. This classroom was going to be Susie's classroom for the next four years. She was filled with anticipation and excitement.

Susie counted forty small light brown wooden desks that was paired with matching chairs. She noticed that the desks had tiny holes, known as inkwells on the right-hand-side of each desk. The desks had lids that one could lift up to place ones Exercise books and crayons. She felt really grown up to have her own desk, and was excited that she would be writing with an ink pen and not a pencil which she had been accustomed to whilst in the nursery.

Susie noticed that the classroom was filled by girls of a similar age as herself. She felt intrigued by the variety of the different complexions of girls. Some of the girls had very pale off-white skin tones, whereas others had pink flushed faces, with brown freckles on their cheeks which Susie didn't possess. Their hair colouring varied from blonde, dark light browns, to black and ginger. Their eye colouring ranged from light brown to blue. This was the first time that Susie really noticed that she looked very different to the white skinned girls in her class. She counted seven girls in her class who looked like herself who had different skin tones ranging from lighter shades of brown to almost ebony.

Susie was approached by her teacher Miss White who was short and plump in stature, wearing a tightly twisted grey bun on the top of her head, which resembled a plumb pudding. Miss White wore a two-toned brown tweed skirt just covering her knees with a matching jacket, revealing a white blouse with a neatly tied bow at the neck. Her shoes resembled her mother's shoes, which was black in colour with a very high heel, with which she struggled to keep a feminine posture whilst walking towards her.

"You sit there, young lady," instructed Miss White, pointing towards the light brown wooden desk, which was in the middle of the classroom, and nestled amongst two regimented desks which were neatly arranged in military symmetry in the classroom. Susie felt intimidated by Miss White's tone of voice and couldn't understand why Miss White was very cold towards her.

Miss White then walked up to Susie when she had settled into her seat and commented,

"Your hair looks very elastic. Does it rebound if I were to tug on it?" asked Miss White as she proceeded to tug at one of Susie's single plaited hair.

"Oh, it does," chortled Miss White as she continued to pull and tug at Susie's hair.

"Ow, ow, ow," screamed Susie. "That hurts!" Protested Susie.

"No, it doesn't Susie!" Exclaimed Miss White. "You're just being silly. I don't want any nonsense from you."

Susie felt deflated by her teacher Miss White's behaviour towards her. She was very sensitive about anyone touching her hair, which brought back nightmarish memories when she was placed in Local Authority Care with her siblings when she was four years old, when her hair was cut short on the first day of her arrival at the Children's Home in Northampton.

Susie knew, however, that school life would be entirely different to her home life because she was aware that the teachers could not beat her or make her feel frightened and vulnerable as her dominating father Mr Solomon Fletcher had made her to feel over the seven years of her short life. She was determined that she would enjoy her time at school, where her mischievous personality and behaviour would be able to run free rein without anyone to control her. She loved to giggle at school and at the wrong time and places, namely the classroom, which would have a detrimental effect on her learning.

Susie's Primary School was streamed in terms of ability ranging from A-C. She was a bright child and so was placed in the 'A' Class which delighted her immensely. She was determined to be the brightest amongst her peers. However, to what lengths she would go to make her high aspirations a reality, was even a surprise to herself.

There was a competitive game that had been going on for a number of years in Susie's Class 1A, which her teacher Miss White decided to test out on Susie's first day at her Primary School. It was called the 'Card Game', which involved her teacher asking the pupils 'General Knowledge' questions. Each pupil's desk had the names of each child who was sitting at their own desk in ascending order, from 1 to 40, which was the number of girls in Susie's class. Whenever a pupil answered the most correct general knowledge questions, the pupil would graduate to the front of the class and would be deemed to be the brightest pupil in the class. Susie loved the card game which allowed her to show off her wide knowledge in various subjects, such as spelling and the 'Times Table', which ranged from the 1 times table right up to the twelve times table. Miss Wright would test the pupils' knowledge of their times tables, by asking them randomly,

"What's 3x5?"

Susie was very smart at playing the card games, which gave her recognition amongst her peers and a formidable force to be reckoned with. After the pupils had been tested on their general knowledge of the card game, Miss White decided that the girls had deserved a well-earned break. Susie decided that she would stay behind whilst the other pupils went into the Dinner Hall to drink their milk from small glass bottles, which was delivered to the school in large plastic crates. Susie was excused and given permission by Miss White from joining the other pupils in the Dinner Hall, because she had a great repulsion for milk, especially cold milk.

The pupils noisily left the classroom, for their short break, followed by Miss White who placed her right plump index finger towards her chubby red lips.

"Ssh, ssh" Miss White commanded. "The other classes are still working."

When Susie felt that her peers and Miss White had gone into the Dinner Hall, she proceeded to rearrange the cards which had the pupils' names written on them and hastily moved the cards which were near to the back of the class to the front, and vice versa. Within a short space of time, she had rearranged a number of her peers named cards on different desks. She told herself that she had morals and decided that she wouldn't move her own card which was placed 10th in rank order in the class of forty girls. Susie found it very difficult to keep a straight face when the girls came back to the classroom to find to their disbelief and horror that their cards with their names on, had mysteriously been moved around on the desks in ascending and descending order. Miss White gave Susie a knowing look and said to her sternly,

"I hope that we won't be having any trouble from you, Madam."

Susie stared at her teacher with a half-smile looking down at her black ill-fitted shoes, which she swung back and forth whilst sitting on her chair next to her school desk.

"Now girls," – Miss White announced suddenly – "the school will be having a West Indian Choir. All the West Indian girls in the school will be required to attend choir practice twice a week in the mornings to sing, 'religious songs' with a Caribbean twist."

There were seven brown looking girls in Susie's class. She was horrified. She didn't want to leave her lessons to sing in the choir. She had high ambitions to learn and didn't want to be away from her class. In fact, if the truth be known, Susie didn't identify herself as being Caribbean. Her mother had always brought her and her siblings up to believe that they were English, and certainly not Caribbean, because she was born in Northampton, and not Jamaica in the Caribbean. The identity of the Fletcher children was a bone of contention between Susie's parents, with her father Mr Solomon Fletcher telling Susie's mother that the Fletcher children were Jamaican.

Now that Susie was in Form 1A, she would stay in her classroom with the rest of her peers for four years before moving on to the local Birmingham Comprehensive School when she reached 11 years old.

She was a mischievous child whilst at St Augustine's Primary School, and according to her teacher Miss White, her 'cards were marked', warning her that she would not be allowed to disrupt her class with her playful antics. However, Susie had her own views on that. She felt that she was able to do what she wanted whilst at school and was free from the shackles of her restrictive home life which was controlled by her dominating father. Although the teachers could hand out corporal punishment in the form of the 'cane', which was a long light-coloured bamboo looking wooden stick, it was in no way feared by Susie, in comparison to the thick black industrial belt that her father had used to beat her. In fact, the cane was rained down on the tips of one's fingers for insolence and for breaking one of the school's mandatory rules such as stealing from another pupil. In any event, Susie confidently thought that if she was 'lucky enough' to be the recipient of getting ten stripes of the cane, it wouldn't hurt half as much as being beaten by her father Mr Solomon Fletcher, who would use every sinew in his body to rein the lashes down onto Susie's slight thin frame which would buckle under the pressure of her father's ferocious onslaught. She hardly ever cried no matter how much she was hurting. She was determined that her father would not have the pleasure or satisfaction in knowing that he had hurt her. Oh no, she wouldn't let on that her body ached for days after getting a beating. Instead, she would clench her muscles in her body which had the effect of reducing the immediate pain. However, Susie's stubbornness to show weakness, made her father all the more determined to break Susie's spirit, which she held onto regardless of the pain that she was going through emotionally.

Indeed, school was a place where she felt that she could do exactly what she wanted to do, and she was determined that no one was going to stand in her way, even if that meant suffering the wroth of her teachers, by being excluded from her classroom, or having the threat of being caned with 'ten of the best', from her teacher Miss White.

Susie's school day went by very quickly and before she could say 'Jack Robinson', she was running through the school gate to where her mother was waiting for her, along with the other parents who had brought along their younger children in prams, pushing them backwards and forwards gently as they chatted away to each other, oblivious that their children were pouring out of the school gate like 'runny treacle' being poured out of a jar.

"Mammie! Mammie!" Susie screamed as she ran towards her mother. She blurted out before her mother could say a word, "I'm in the 'A class' at school with the other bright girls!" She exclaimed excitedly.

"That's really lovely Susie," replied her mother who was holding baby Benjamin precariously with one arm, whilst Susie was tugging at her mother's skirt and wanting to be hugged and congratulated.

"Be careful Susie," Mrs Ruby Fletcher warned. "I'm holding baby Benjamin and I can't pick you up at the same time. Wait until we get home, and I will be able to give you a big hug."

Susie wasn't impressed or pleased that her mother couldn't place baby Benjamin onto the ground whilst her mother gave her a hug. Baby Benjamin was now a toddler and she thought that he still received too much attention from her mother.

Susie's mischievous, stubborn and rebellious nature at school was to get her into further trouble at St Augustine's Primary School. On one of the many such occasions, she deliberated about playing a prank on her teacher Miss White, who she had grown to dislike immensely. Her memory took her back to her first encounter with her teacher when she pulled her hair out of curiosity because she was curious to know as to whether her hair was similar to an elastic band if pulled. She not only found her new teacher's behaviour unacceptable, but she thought that her teacher was poking fun and demeaning her in the presence of the other pupils. Her mother Mrs Ruby Fletcher had lovingly combed and divided her thick black bushy hair into six plaits, with three plaits situated at the front of her long narrow face, with the other three plaits situated at the top and back of her small head. Susie hated having her hair plaited and shunned the attention that her teacher Miss White was giving to her plaits.

Her teacher Miss White would sit at the front of the class and would read to the class of forty girls every afternoon before the end of the school day. Miss White would be perched on a high legged dark oak chair with a brown cushion, which Susie thought was to make up for her lack of height, rather than for comfort. Her desk was also made of dark oak, which was held up with four very long legs. Her high desk conveniently had the advantage of allowing her teacher to see what every pupil was doing in the classroom, much to Susie's displeasure and frustration. Miss White would bend the book back as she turned each page. Susie would invariably be daydreaming and half-paying attention during her teacher's afternoon story telling.

On one particular afternoon, whilst her teacher Miss White was reading a story to the class of forty girls about how children lived in the Victorian times, with poverty being responsible for the high incidence of childhood mortality, Susie hatched a plan to make her teacher literally jump out of her seat. Miss White would intermittently peer over her metal rimmed glasses which had strings attached to make sure that Susie was paying attention.

Miss White concluded her reading by telling the class how lucky they all were, to be living in the twentieth century and not in the Victorian times.

When the class went out to play at break-time she hatched a plan to place drawing pins and sharp rose thorns onto her teacher's chair. Susie had collected a dozen thorns the previous day whilst out in the playground at lunch time and had sneakily placed them in her desk. She had collected the drawing pins from the large cupboard that was situated in the far corner at the back of her classroom.

Susie hastily ran up to Miss White's high oak chair and scattered the thorns and drawing pins onto her teacher's brown cushion. Surely her teacher wouldn't notice the array of drawing pins and thorns which had been placed onto her chair.

When the girls returned to the classroom after ten minutes, she waited with bated breath as Miss White walked towards her chair and sat down onto her chair. Susie looked directly at her teacher, but she was disappointed that the objects that she had placed onto her teacher's chair didn't have the desired effect of making her teacher literally jump out of her seat. Instead, her teacher knowingly looked directly at Susie without letting on to the rest of the class that Susie was the pupil responsible for placing the sharp objects onto her chair.

Chapter 17

History Repeats Itself in the Fletchers' Household

As Susie became older and had almost reached the age of 11 years old and was looking to move on from St Augustine's Primary School, her dysfunctional home life had taken its toll on her. She began to dread coming home from school and would find any reason to avoid being in the family home any more than she needed to be. She decided that she would get involved in afterschool team sports such as Netball which involved several afterschool Netball practices and matches against the local Primary schools across Birmingham. She asked her Netball teacher Mrs Hanson to visit the family home to get permission for she to join her School's Netball Team.

Susie's netball teacher Mrs Hanson made a visit to the family home, to get her father's permission for her to play in her school's netball team, which would involve her having to stay on at the school for a few hours at the end of the school day several evenings a week.

"Netball will be good for Susie," said Mrs Hanson persuasively. "It will boost her confidence and give her a sense of independence and allow her to be less clingy to her mother."

Susie's father was not swayed by Mrs Hanson's reasonings to allow her to play in her school's netball team, but responded to Mrs Hanson by saying,

"I'm only allowing her to attend netball training afterschool in her last year in Primary School at St Augustine's because when she attends Birmingham Comprehensive School, she will need to put her head to her lessons and concentrate on her education."

Mrs Hanson knew not to argue with Mr Solomon Fletcher and accepted his illogical reasoning with gratitude that Susie would be able to spend some well-needed time out of the family home.

Mr Solomon Fletcher continued to rule the Fletcher family including Susie's mother Mrs Ruby Fletcher with a rod of iron. Mrs Ruby Fletcher didn't have a say in any important family decisions.

During the time that Susie's teacher was talking with Susie's father, her mother was prevented by her husband from giving her views or opinions on what was best for their daughter, even though she was present during the conversation between Mrs Hanson and her husband.

Susie became more withdrawn in the family home and there was very little interaction between Susie and her father. In fact, she had stopped having any dialogue with her father and only spoke to her father when she arrived home from school.

"Good evening, Daddy," she would say to Mr Solomon Fletcher, when she entered the family home. Her father wouldn't acknowledge his daughter's greeting but would look menacingly at her and would shout,

"What have I told you that you should look at me when you come through di door?" Her father would shout, rising from his chair as Susie slipped past him and into the living room before he could scold her any further.

"I'm talking to you Susie!" Mr Solomon Fletcher shouted. "Come here! I'm going to give you a beating for your very disrespectful behaviour."

"I've been watching you for the last few weeks and there's only one man and one woman in this house."

"Come here Susie," her father shouted.

Susie by now, had run up the steep bare dark wooden stairs and into her sparsely decorated bedroom, which consisted of a low brown metal bed with a thin springless double mattress with a dark brown heavy headboard which she shared with her younger sister Ruby. She franticly proceeded to put on several layers of clothing, including thick jumpers, dresses and two layers of thick green woollen tights which transformed her thin wiry frame giving the appearance of a stuffed 'Guy Fawkes', which the children in the area where she lived, would push along the dark streets in old, dilapidated push chairs that had been discarded.

Susie had learned from experience to protect herself in this way because she had suffered endless years of beatings at the hands of her violent father who had 'put the fear of God' into her, which left her wishing that she could one day escape the endless beatings.

As Susie arrived downstairs and opened the door which led into the dimly lit living room, her father Mr Solomon Fletcher was seated on a dilapidated large grey settee. The heat from the raging open coal fire belched out cinders onto the fireplace.

"I'm going to teach you a lesson to have manners!" Shouted Mr Fletcher as he stood up and walked towards Susie. His tall broad frame towered over Susie as she began to tremble because she knew what would befall her.

As her father reined blow after blow with the grey thick and heavy leather belt upon her frail and fragile body, Susie defended her body from the onslaught of the beatings which were coming thick and fast, by deflecting the lashes with quick and precise arm movements. She refused to cry whilst her father was beating her which infuriated Mr Solomon Fletcher.

"Take off those clothes," demanded her father. Susie began to tremble because she knew that the beatings would hurt her badly if she took off the extra layers of clothing.

"Take them off now," her father shouted, pointing to Susie's bulky clothing.

As Susie proceeded to take off the extra layers of clothing, with just her thin yellow cotton dress above her knees and sockless feet, her father walked over to a small door in the corner of the dimly lit living room which led to the cellar. Mr Solomon Fletcher descended hastily into the cellar, and down its jagged brick steps where the family's coal was kept. The coal was delivered by the Coalmen once a week and poured down the grate from the pavement outside, and through a grate that was lifted. The fuse to the house was situated in the belly of the cellar. Susie noticed that the house had suddenly plunged into utter pitch darkness as her father switched off the lighting to the whole house.

Susie froze in fear of what was to come next. She was subjected to the worse beatings that she had ever experienced with the whole house in darkness, as her father crept up from behind her, and reined blow after blow onto her defenceless fragile body. Her screams for her father to stop the beatings fell on deaf ears. The beatings only stopped when the neighbour from next door Mrs Hickory banged on the front door shouting,

"I'm going to report you to Social Services for beating your children!" Mrs Hickory remonstrated to Susie's father.

The intense fear which took hold of Susie on that fateful evening had a long-term effect on her relationship with her father, which had cascaded into an all-time low. She ceased all verbal communications with her father which resulted in further friction and tension in the Fletcher household. Mrs Ruby Fletcher carried the burden of the gradual disintegration of her family and bared the brunt of the family's downward spiral. The outside world oblivious to the emotional, psychological and physical violence within the Fletcher family's four walls.

Chapter 18

Susie Goes Missing After School

It was on a rainy dismal day that Susie decided to run away from home. She had arrived at school rather earlier than the usual with her mother at 8:40 because her mother had to take most of the morning off from work to attend the local Birmingham Women's Hospital as her mother had mentioned that she was having 'women's problem'. She had overheard her mother mention to her father early one morning several days ago whilst her parents were downstairs in the kitchen. Susie had no idea what 'Women's problem' meant and had the presence of mind in not asking her mother what this meant, just in case Mrs Ruby Fletcher would scold her by telling her that this was grown-up conversations between herself and Mr Solomon Fletcher which didn't concern her.

Her mother hastily half kissed her on the cheek at the school gate, rushing off in the process, and giving muffled instructions to Susie.

"Work hard at school today, Susie. I will be twenty minutes late collecting you from school because I will need to make up my hours at work. Wait for me in your classroom," instructed Mrs Ruby Fletcher.

She watched her mother dash across the busy congested road which was littered with large vehicles and buses ferrying exhausted looking men in blackened cloth caps and dark brown 'donkey jackets', to their respective places of work. The buses belched out black fumes into the air which reduced visibility even further for the drivers on this bleak mid-winter morning.

Susie looked longingly and lovingly at her mother with the knowledge that she wouldn't be going home after school. She had made up her mind that she wouldn't be meeting her mother at the end the school day and wouldn't be going home with her after school. It didn't even cross Susie's mind about the upset or worry that her running away would have on her mother and her siblings. She knew that her father would not be affected by her absence from the family home. Indeed, Susie felt that her father would be relieved if he never saw her or set eyes on her again.

Susie spent her day at school being present in body, but her mind was not on her schoolwork, and in particular spelling and preparation for the Christmas upcoming school play in the next four weeks. She had been given a part in introducing the audience (which would include the children's parents being in attendance) to 'The Nativity', which she was looking forward to taking part in, had she not had so much on her mind.

"Are you paying attention Susie?" Her teacher Miss White snapped.

"You will need to ask your mother to help you to practice your lines at home because you haven't been your lively mischievous self over the last few weeks," commented Miss White.

Susie didn't reply to her teacher's observations but pinched her thin wiry legs in order to prevent herself from bursting into tears. She wanted to confide in her teacher about the beatings that she was suffering at the hands of her father and about the regular beatings that her mother and siblings were also subjected to. Susie knew that disclosing what went on at home would not change anything at home, for her nor her family. In fact, she felt that her disclosure to Miss White would make things far worse for her, and she feared that she would be subjected to further and more severe beatings at the hands of her father.

Over the years Susie had thought that there wasn't a way out of this madness and that she didn't have any other choice or option but to 'shut up and put up' with the beatings at the hands of her father. It hadn't crossed her mind that she would grow up one day, and that the beatings wouldn't last forever.

Susie had a best friend called Grace with whom she had grown very close to whilst at St Augustine's Primary School. She hatched up a plan that at the end of the school day she would tell Grace that her parents had agreed for her go home with her to play, and that her mother who was working late, would fetch her from Grace's house. Grace was given far more freedom and independence than Susie because she was allowed by her parents to walk to and from school which was roughly around ten minutes away from school. In contrast, Susie lived just around the corner from school, but her mother would hold her hand whilst taking her to school. Susie envied her friend Grace because she was always happy and appeared not to have a care in the world. Grace came from a family of eight girls and one boy.

Grace was the opposite to Susie in stature, and was very plump and short in stature, and a little shorter than Susie, with very short tight black curly hair. She had a very dark brown complexion with dark brown almost black eyes which twinkled when she laughed.

At the end of the school day Susie told Grace her parents had given permission for her to accompany her home to her house, and that her mother would fetch her later in the evening from Grace's house, because she had gone into work late and so would be finishing work later in the evening.

"That's great Susie!" Grace screamed in excitement.

"We can play skipping and 'two-ballers'."

Two-ballers was a game that the older girls at St Augustine's School had taught the younger girls in the school. This game involved using two soft rubber assorted coloured balls which was thrown against a wall and caught with either hand, whilst singing a song at the same time. Whoever dropped a ball would hand both balls to the other girl who was waiting to take their turn at repeating the same process. Susie loved the two-ballers game. One of Susie's favourite songs that she would sing whilst playing two-ballers, went along the lines of,

What do you do with the drunken Sailor?

What do you do with the drunken Sailor?

What do you do with the drunken Sailor?

Early in the morning,

Way-hay and up she rises,

Way-hay and up she rises,

Way-hay and up she rises,

Early in the morning.

Put him in the long boat till he's sober,

Put him in the long boat till he's sober,

Put him in the long boat till he's sober,

Early in the morning.

As Susie and Grace walked along the cobbled streets towards Grace's home, Susie was struck by the similarity of the cobbled streets that led to her own home. As she approached Grace's house, it struck her that she may never go home again and a tinge of sadness overwhelmed her for a fleeting moment, which passed swiftly when the recent memories of the traumatic experiences that she had endured going back as far as she could remember, at the hands her father Mr Solomon Fletcher. The memories of her traumatic experiences came flooding back and jumped back into the forefront of her mind like a 'Jack in a box'. She decided that she did have a choice, and that she wasn't going to put up with the beatings any longer.

Grace excitedly ran down the narrow-cobbled entry which led to her house, with Susie in tow, and through the tall rickety back dilapidated wooden brown gate, which was half hanging off at the hinges.

"Good evening, Mama," Grace said excitedly as she ran in through the unlocked back door which led into the small dark kitchen inside her house.

Grace's surname was Jones, and so Susie addressed Grace's mother as Mrs Jones, which Susie had been taught by her parents as good manners.

"Good evening, Mrs Jones," said Susie in an almost scripted manner.

"Good evening, Susie," replied Mrs Jones.

"Does your mother Mrs Fletcher know that you're here?" Mrs Jones asked inquisitively.

"Yes, she does," replied Grace hastily, preventing Susie from responding to Mrs Jones question.

"I was asking Susie, not you Grace."

"It's bad manners to interrupt whilst I'm talking to Susie," said Mrs Jones scoldingly to Grace.

"Yes, she knows that I'm here," replied Susie confidently.

"She had an appointment at the hospital this morning and so she's working late. She told me that I could go home with Grace after school. My teacher Miss White knows that I would be walking with Grace to her house."

"That's good Susie," replied Mrs Jones, reassured at Susie's lengthy and plausible explanation.

"As long as the school and your parents know that you're here, I'm happy with that."

"Make yourself at home," Mrs Jones said kindly.

Susie was relieved that Mrs Jones didn't press her for any further information because she felt that she would probably burst into tears, due to Grace's mother's gentle and caring disposition. She longed to confide in someone about the internal pain that she was going through, and she felt that Grace's mother would've been an ideal trustful person in which to pour out her sorrow and sadness.

Grace's mother resembled Grace in every way, although her skin tone was of a lighter caramel complexion. She was plump in stature, wearing a yellow flowery dress with a blue apron tied across her wide frame. She wore a flowery coloured scarf, tied tightly across her large forehead, with an array of short plaits scattered at the edges where her scarf hadn't covered.

Grace's father worked during the day and hadn't returned home from work, whilst Grace's mother worked nights at the local factory to support their family of eleven.

"Let's play two-ballers," said Grace excitedly, whilst Mrs Jones prepared the family's evening meal.

"I will be going to work soon Grace," shouted her mother from the kitchen window.

"I hope that Susie's mother fetches her before I leave for work because I would like to have a word with her."

Susie's heart sank at Mrs Jones sudden revelation. *What would she want to speak to my mother about?* She thought.

"Are you coming to play two-ballers Susie," Grace shouted.

"Yes, lets," replied Susie excitedly.

The two best friends went into the wide bricked garden to play, with both girls each holding two blue and red soft balls between them.

After what seemed like hours playing two-ballers in the garden, Susie and Grace went back into the house to have their evening meal that Mrs Jones had prepared for her husband Mr Vincent Jones and their nine children. The family came together to eat their evening meal in the small family dining room which had an uncanny resemblance to Susie's house. There was a well-established open raging fire with a fire guard around it, which had the family's clothes drying slowly, with steam rising from the dripping garments. On the wall was a picture frame with a black and white photograph of Mr and Mrs Jones with their nine children, who all stood next to each other in ascending order of age. What struck Susie was that all the family members were smiling and looked really happy.

So that's where Grace gets that look from, as though she hasn't a care in the world, Susie thought.

All nine siblings, eight girls and one boy, plus Susie sat squashed together, shoulder to shoulder around the large dark brown dining room table, to eat their evening meal which consisted of a watery spicy soup, added with tightly kneaded corn meal dumplings, sweet potatoes, unripened green bananas and yams, which resembled the inside of a tree bark. This variety of food was the staple of many West Indian families in the UK. One could hear a pin drop as the family dipped their heads down in unison with their table spoons into their large soup bowls, slurping the hot spicy soup.

After the family had eaten their evening meal Susie took Grace aside and told her that her mother wasn't going to fetch her from her house as she had led her to believe, but that she had run away from home.

"What are you going to do?" Grace asked in shock and disbelief.

"Can I stay at your house tonight?" asked Susie.

Grace hesitated and thought for a moment, and then said,

"I've got an idea," said Grace hopping on one leg, which she would invariably do when she was excited.

"Why don't you pretend that your mother has fetched you, and then come back into the house through the front door?"

"You could then go upstairs into my bedroom and hide in the wardrobe. You could then slip into our bed with my seven sisters. I will find a white head scarf for you to wear, so that when my Mama comes home in the morning after her night shift, you can hide in the wardrobe before she comes into our bedroom which she does most mornings to get us ready for school."

113

With both girls having agreed on a plan of action, Susie began to feel less anxious about being found out. She certainly didn't want to return home ever again.

Her mind was finally made up. She decided that she never wanted to see her father Mr Solomon Fletcher ever again. However, she was conflicted because she desperately wanted to be with her mother and siblings, but she was unable to work out how this would be possible with her father in the midst of it all. Her mind started to play tricks on her. *Maybe she would be able to see her family again if her father was sent a Telegram that his mother was very ill and close to death*, she thought. Her father was very close to his mother, being the youngest child. She remembered her father having one of those emergency Telegrams when she was in St Augustine's Primary School, when her father was told that he needed to travel to Jamaica immediately because his mother, who he adoringly called 'Old Agatha', was ill and he needed to travel to Jamaica as soon he could book a flight. Susie remembered being overjoyed because her father was away from the family home for what seemed like eternity. She recalled her mother telling her that her father would be in Jamaica for four months. Four months to Susie sounded like eternity. She recollected the freedom that the Fletcher children had when their father went to Jamaica was indescribable. In actual fact, Susie had prayed that her father stayed in Jamaica for good and never came back to the UK to disturb her newfound freedom. Life without her father was liberating. Everything around her looked and sounded so different. She even noticed the birds singing, which see had never noticed before. Life had colour and was radiant and lacked the overcast foreboding feeling that she felt when her father was in the family home.

Susie was brought back to the reality of the present moment when Grace, in hushed tones nervously asked her,

"Are you going to leave the house now through the back gate?"

"Then come back through the front door where I will take you upstairs into the bedroom that I share with my seven sisters," Grace continued.

"Okay I will do that," Susie replied, uncertain as to whether Grace's plan would backfire on them. She certainly didn't want to get Grace into trouble with her lovely parents.

Susie was able to carry out Grace's plan with exact precision and was ushered upstairs into Grace's bedroom, which bore similarities with her own bedroom which she shared with her younger sister Ruby. She was mesmerised and struck by the bottled green 'Water Babies', full length curtains, which covered the length of the sash windows. The 'Water Babies' curtain designs depicted babies swimming without a care in the world in a sea of bright blue water with an array of seashells and colourful plant fauna, in reds, pinks, greens and purples.

"You need to stay in this wardrobe until bedtime," insisted Grace.

The thought of hiding in the wardrobe brought in tinge of excitement to her. The wardrobe was 'humungous', she thought.

Susie was overwhelmed and in awe of the tall dark brown antique wardrobe. Behind the two thick wardrobe doors, the clothes rail was filled with the Jones sisters' clothes.

As she stepped into the wardrobe she was reminded of C.S Lewis's fantasy novel, 'The Loin, the Witch, and the Wardrobe'. She hid behind the dense clothing in complete dread and anticipation, hoping that she would not be found in the wardrobe by Grace's mother.

Later in the evening Susie heard Grace whisper to her through the dense undergrowth of clothing that it was now safe for her to come out of the wardrobe.

"I've found a spare headscarf that you can wear," whispered Grace.

"Mama has gone to work now, so you can come out of the wardrobe and sleep in the middle between me and my sisters," she whispered.

The bed was a large King size bed that Susie would be sharing with Grace and her seven sisters ranging in ages from 8 to 16 years. The mattress was covered with an off-white cotton sheet, with several layers of brown heavy blankets. A dark wooden headboard graced the top of the bed.

Susie timidly stepped out of the wardrobe and into the dimly lit room.

"You can get into bed now before Daddy comes upstairs to say goodnight to us," Grace told her assuredly.

Snuggled shoulder to shoulder between Grace and her seven siblings Susie wondered whether this is what her teachers meant when they used the expression, 'snuggled together like sardines in a sardine tin'.

To Susie's surprise, Grace's father didn't notice the extra 'white scarfed head' in the bed when he entered the room. In any event, she had fallen asleep as her head had hit the pillow, exhausted from the long day.

Susie was awakened the next morning by the loud shouting of Grace's mother, Mrs Jones.

"Grace! Grace! Grace," she shouted.

"Where is Susie?"

"The Police, Susie's mother Mrs Ruby Fletcher, and a Social Worker are all downstairs."

"They have been looking for her all night because she didn't return home last night."

Susie jolted out of bed and slipped into her ill-fitting squeaky shoes. She was still wearing her school uniform from the day before, that she had slept in, which was now crumpled. She was worried that Grace would now be in a lot of trouble for hiding her in her house overnight. She ran down the dark dusty wooden stairs 'like a bat out of hell', holding onto the dark brown ridged bannister in the process.

Susie entered the small front room which was sparsely furnished with a glass cabinet which exhibited numerous wine glasses, and a small green settee with a plastic covering. A large colourful ornamental fish sat proudly on the windowsill next to the netted curtains. Most West Indian families in the UK would claim ownership of such an ornamental fish in their homes, and Grace's family was of no exception.

A stern looking tanned Policeman was stood next to the entrance to the white front room door. He had what looked like a large, pointed helmet under his right arm. Next to the policeman was Susie's mother Mrs Ruby Fletcher in floods of tears being comforted on the small green settee by a mature looking woman with flushed rosy cheeks. She believed that this woman was the Social Worker that Grace's mother was referring to. The Social Worker was wearing a dark short jacket with a white patterned starched blouse, and a matching long black skirt, finished off with a low-heeled smart pointed black leather shoes.

"Hello Susie, my name is Mrs Marsden. I'm the Social Worker from Birmingham City Council."

"Your mother has been sick with worry about you when you failed to wait for her after school last night," she said firmly but softly.

"The police have been searching high and low for you all night," continued Mrs Marsden pointing to the silent policeman who was standing at the front room door.

"Why did you run away from home Susie?" Mrs Marsden asked gently.

Susie couldn't hold in her emotions any longer and she blurted out the words, like a river that had burst its banks,

"Tell them Mammie," Susie screamed and breathing heavily.

"Tell them that Daddy beats you and beats all the children, including me who he really hates and doesn't want in the family home anymore."

Mrs Ruby Fletcher continued sobbing but didn't reply to Susie's plea.

Susie's wiry frame rocked as she sobbed, her eyes blinded by the rivers of tears pouring uncontrollably from her small eye ducts.

"I'm never going back home to that cruel monster who beats me all the time!" She screamed.

"There, there," said Mrs Marsden in a gentle tone of voice.

"We won't be forcing you back home, Susie. We will be taking you into Local Authority Care today, and you will be placed into a Children's Home in Herefordshire."

CPSIA information can be obtained
at www.ICGtesting.com
Printed in the USA
LVHW020533010322
712195LV00010B/555

9 781398 431461